MURDER IN THE NEWS

A 1920S HISTORICAL COZY MYSTERY - AN EVIE PARKER MYSTERY BOOK 15

SONIA PARIN

Murder in the News Copyright © 2022 Sonia Parin

No part of this publication may be reproduced in any form or by any means, without the prior written permission of the author, except in the case of brief quotations embodied in critical articles and reviews. This is a work of fiction. Names, characters, places and incidents are the product of the author's imagination or are used fictitiously. Any resemblance to actual persons, living or dead, organizations, events or locales is entirely coincidental.
vJune

ISBN: 9798828580354

CHAPTER 1

1922
Outside The Marlborough Head Pub
North Audley Street, Mayfair

In the last hour, Wilfred Greer had seen twenty-seven men he recognized and not one of them had recognized him.

The edge of his lip lifted as he wondered how they would have reacted if he'd approached them.

Not well, not well at all, he thought as he reached the street corner, the perfect spot from which to do some surveillance, he thought and stopped outside the Marlborough Head, using the reflection on the window to pretend to adjust his hat while he observed someone else he recognized crossing the street.

That would make it twenty-eight men he'd recognized and it wasn't even midday. He turned to look down the street just as a young woman tripped out of the pub and nearly collided with him.

Gasping, she apologized and hurried away, crossing the street with barely a glance at the oncoming traffic.

Tipping his hat at her, he then looked down at his watch and calculated the time it would take him to reach his destination.

He had plenty of time, he thought. He would take care of the morning's business and then stop for a spot of lunch. He might even amuse himself by dropping by the club to see how many more men he would recognize and how many would pretend they didn't recognize him.

He turned back to the window to make sure his hat was tilted the way he liked it.

Narrowing his gaze, he smiled and scratched around his mind for the number of people he'd recognized that morning. Twenty-eight.

"Make that twenty-nine."

Meanwhile...
Inside The Marlborough Head Pub
North Audley Street, Mayfair

Evie looked up from her notebook and saw Tom folding his newspaper. He stood up and walked over to join her at her table.

The morning's task had taken longer than expected so she assumed he would be eager to leave.

Reaching for her gloves, she slipped them on. "I'm sorry that took so long. You really should have taken care of your business."

He shook his head and settled in a chair opposite her. "That can wait."

"Are you sure?" Evie assumed it had something to do with his financial interests. However, as far as she knew, they were all back home in America. She also knew her brother took care of Tom's investments. Other than that, she had no knowledge of his business dealings in England or if, indeed, there were any. She only knew he periodically received sealed envelopes and telephone calls which he dealt with in private.

That morning, however, he had asked her about her schedule, something he'd never done before. Prodding him for information, she had discovered he had a matter to attend to. While he had been quite dismissive about it, she knew he was keen to sort something out.

"I hope the newspaper kept you amused. Anything interesting?"

"Nothing world shattering," he offered.

A couple of well-dressed gentlemen walked in and sat at a nearby table. They'd arrived just as the pub had opened and Evie had hoped to have completed her business within a half hour. So far, they had more or less had the place to themselves. Soon, it would fill up for luncheon.

"That's the third lady's maid you've interviewed today," Tom mused. "I take it you won't be hiring her."

"What makes you say that?"

"She hurried out like a bat out of hell, her expression... flustered. So I assume that means she didn't get the job."

It seemed unlikely, Evie thought. "The right one will come along, I'm sure." They had been holding interviews for two days now. While each candidate had offered impeccable references, not a single one had displayed the strength of character Evie had been searching for.

Tom raised his eyebrows. "From where I sat, she appeared to be perfectly fine. Then again, I don't know what you and Millicent are looking for…"

Evie didn't wish to offer an explanation. It would simply take too long. Needless to say, a lady's maid would be privy to her private life.

Evie was prepared to spend some time nurturing the relationship. However, first, she needed to find someone who showed promise of fitting in.

She'd enjoyed a special relationship with Caro, her first lady's maid. Before Millicent had taken over from Caro, she had been her second lady's maid. Now, of course, Millicent had stepped into the role of secretary.

Glancing out the window to look at the passersby, Evie explained, "She didn't feel right. Perhaps I failed to set her at ease. The poor girl fidgeted throughout the entire interview and told me she found the questions difficult to follow and understand. I kept them simple but, honestly, how simple is simple?"

"Countess, not everyone has the ability to understand and follow convoluted dialogue."

Sounding affronted, Evie gasped, "Convoluted? Did you not hear me say I kept the questions simple?"

Tom smiled. "Sometimes, your imagination runs away with you and people struggle to keep up. Remember, the average person is only comfortable with what they know." Tom tilted his head and studied her for a moment. "Let me guess, you set a hypothetical scenario and asked her how she would react."

She had, but only because Millicent had urged her to do so.

Evie looked down at Holmes and gave him a playful scratch under his chin.

Millicent had even provided a set of questions formulated to test the candidate's willingness to adapt to new and ever-changing circumstances.

While initially reluctant to employ such a tactic, in the end, Evie had relented and had even found Millicent's idea to be quite marvelous. So much so, she had added a few questions of her own to test the young woman's imagination.

Nothing too demanding, she insisted.

Tom smiled and shook his head.

"What?"

"You must have frightened the poor woman."

"I couldn't have."

"Are you sure?"

Evie lifted her chin. "You must admit, life at Halton House or, for that matter, Woodridge House, *indeed*, wherever we might find ourselves, can be and usually is quite strange. I merely tried to place the candidate in the midst of one of our average days. You know very well we could be enjoying a quiet moment in the library and, suddenly, the doors will burst open and Henrietta will march right in, strike up a regal pose, and announce the sky has turned a disturbing shade of green."

Tom did a very good job of hiding his smile. "Green?"

Evie gave a vigorous nod. "Actually, green with purple dots."

Tom tipped his head back and laughed.

"You know precisely what I mean." Evie shrugged. "If it's not a case of someone barging in, we are lured toward some strange occurrence within the household, which invariably leads us straight to trouble. Do you know, there are times when I dread the arrival of the mail, especially missives addressed to someone else in the house."

His eyes twinkled. "Henrietta, Toodles... Or Sara?"

"You find this amusing." She had merely wanted to see if the prospective lady's maid could deal with unusual circumstances. Right then, an image formed in her mind of Lotte Mannering walking in dressed as a scullery maid. The lady detective had been known to use all manner of disguises. What would a lady's maid not used to such goings on do?

Then, there were other factors to consider...

Evie leaned in and whispered, "Yesterday, I heard Henrietta complain about the drudgery of town life and this happened directly after one of her visitors left." Evie knew the moment Henrietta got a bee in her bonnet, her new lady's maid would be exposed to who knew what and she needed to know she had the disposition to cope well with it all.

Tom smiled. "Henrietta's visitor must have been very dull."

Evie's voice hitched, "It was Lady Farnsworth. She always delivers a full account of what everyone has been doing and the full account leaves absolutely nothing out. Henrietta has always found her highly entertaining. Yet, there she was, complaining of boredom."

"I thought you said she complained about the drudgery of town life."

"Yes, and that equates to Henrietta being utterly bored. Do you see what I mean?"

Tom pretended to look quite serious. "Oh, Yes. Yes, I see."

"Do you? Can you see the full picture?"

"Give me a moment." He closed his eyes and smiled. "Oh, yes. Yes, yes. I see it." Opening his eyes, he asked, "When the young woman's head stopped spinning, was she able to answer you?"

Evie huffed out a breath and sat back. "I believe we have strayed. As I said, I kept my questions simple. She must have been overcome with nerves. From the moment she sat down, she did not stop looking at her wristwatch."

"Perhaps she sneaked out to see you and feared her employer would discover she was looking for another position. She might be working for a harpy who spends her days pursing her lips, tapping her foot in exasperation and being thoroughly monstrous to her servants."

"Her references were impeccable. The woman she works for is about to travel and…" Evie looked down at a notebook in front of her, "Merrin, that's the lady's maid, doesn't wish to leave England. She doesn't trust foreigners."

"Oh." Tom looked away to hide his smile. "Perhaps that's why she was so nervous with you. After all, you sound like a foreigner."

The thought hadn't even crossed her mind.

"What nonsense," Evie declared.

No, she would not do, Evie thought. She wouldn't last a day in her household. Heavens, what would she make of the daily upheavals?

Millicent had repeatedly warned her it would not be

easy to fill the position and now Evie found herself in complete agreement.

While they needed someone special, Evie would settle for someone with an open mind. Actually, she rather liked the idea of employing someone with an active imagination. At the very least, she needed someone who could follow a simple conversation without her mind wandering off.

Halfway through the interview, she'd wanted to snap at the young woman and tell her to *keep up*.

"It's possible she found the setting uncomfortable." Tom glanced around the Mayfair pub. "You must admit, interviewing the candidates in a pub is highly unusual."

Evie shrugged. "It makes perfect sense." At least, it did to her new secretary, she thought.

Holding the interviews at the pub had been yet another one of Millicent's bright ideas, saying a pub would make it easier to test if the candidates had any bad habits such as being distracted by passersby, specifically young men who might lead them astray.

In Evie's opinion, what her new lady's maid did in her private time was entirely her business, but Millicent had argued right back, insisting the candidates were more likely to relax and let their guards down in a public space, thereby exposing their true natures.

While Millicent had settled into her new role of secretary with admirable aplomb, she had insisted on remaining as her lady's maid, saying they should take the time to ensure they selected the perfect fit or, heaven help them, they risked exposing the entire household to who knew what...

Evie joined Tom in gazing out the window.

"I must say, life with you is never going to be dull," Tom mused. "I suppose it's easier to go along with Millicent's ideas than to do battle against her reasoning."

Evie nodded in agreement. "There are times when my life feels like a whirlpool. My lady's maid needs to have a grounding effect on me." Picking up her fountain pen, she uncapped it and made a quick note.

Tom leaned in and looked at her list of questions. "Are you adding to the criteria?"

In her opinion, Evie was simplifying the list.

She underlined the word 'uncomplicated' and looked up. "You know my mind tends to wander. I can't have a lady's maid who suffers from the same affliction. She must be focused and have a sharp mind." Evie pushed out an exasperated sigh. "I'm sure we'll find the right lady's maid well before Henrietta finds a way to secure a title for you."

Tom shrugged. "Henrietta hasn't said anything in a long while. I suspect she has given up all hope."

"This is not something you can acquire through a catalogue." Evie's smile seemed to hold a multitude of secrets and insights. "I'm disappointed in you, Mr. Winchester. I thought you could see past her pretense."

After a moment, Tom blinked. "What are you saying?"

Evie smiled. "Henrietta hasn't given up, she is merely biding her time. As I've said before, I suspect she might have encountered a slight glitch. You shouldn't mistake her silence for defeat. In your place, I would practice answering to Sir Tom. Or will it be Sir Thomas?"

Tom crossed his arms. "And, in the event we finally tie the knot, how will you be addressed?"

"Me?" Evie waved her hand. "I'll be Lady Winchester.

Oh, that has rather a nice ring to it. I'll have to ask Henrietta for clarification, but I suspect I will be able to style myself as Lady Winchester, the Countess of Woodridge." Evie gave him an impish smile as she teased him, "It has something to do with marrying beneath me. Then again, I came by the title through my marriage, so it might not apply. In which case, you'll be thankful for small mercies."

"I'm not sure I'll be able to stop calling you Countess." He drummed his fingers on the table. "Are you interviewing any other candidates today?"

"No, that was the last one for today." Evie looked around the pub. Spotting Millicent, she beckoned her over.

Millicent put away her notebook, gathered her handbag, and approached her.

"Well, Millicent? What did you think?" Evie asked.

Her secretary shook her head. "That last one only had eyes for Mr. Winchester."

Evie looked surprised. Millicent had suggested placing herself at a discreet distance so she could observe the interview. "How could you tell? You were sitting all the way in the corner."

Millicent smiled and tapped her nose. "My intuition, milady. It always serves me well. She kept her gaze on you, while darting glances at Mr. Winchester who, at the time, happened to be the only man in the pub."

"Millicent, at some point we will have to give someone the benefit of the doubt."

Millicent glanced at Tom. "Milady, I always feel it's best to be safe than sorry." Lowering her voice, she whispered, "I have heard too many stories about lady's maids taking liberties they shouldn't… If you know what I mean."

Evie trusted Tom implicitly and she had become accustomed to women always looking at him, but she would reserve her argument for another time.

"There's no hurry, milady. I haven't made my decision lightly." She dug inside her handbag and produced an envelope. "Edmonds delivered this while you were interviewing Merrin Smith."

"What is it?"

"It's a report compiled by Lotte Mannering. She looked into the candidates. The only one who caught her attention was Merrin Smith. During the last week, she spent every night at the pub. That tells me she has nothing better to do with her evenings. Also, she is obviously used to having her evenings off. You must admit that is highly unusual. We're lucky to get a half day off a week. Of course, her employer might not need her every night." Millicent pursed her lips. "I don't wish to pass judgment, milady." Brightening, she added, "Tomorrow promises to be a better day." She put away the envelope, checked her watch and nodded. "I should return to Woodridge House. The agency might have sent a message about some more candidates."

Tom waited for Millicent to walk out of the pub to lean forward and murmur, "She's relishing her new role. It's almost frightening."

"Just be glad Millicent is not interviewing you for your role as my future husband."

Tom adjusted his tie. "On that note, I think a walk will do us good." He picked up his hat and newspaper and, looking up, he stilled.

Evie followed the direction of his gaze. "What is it?"

He was looking out the window and, she thought, straight at a man who stood at the curb, ready to cross the street.

Someone he recognized?

"Tom?"

He turned to her and smiled. "Let's take a walk."

CHAPTER 2

*I*nstead of heading toward Woodridge House, Tom signaled in the opposite direction.

Evie saw the man who had captured Tom's attention cross the street and wondered if Tom would suggest crossing the street to follow him.

He didn't.

Instead, they continued walking, matching the man's pace. When he slowed, they slowed down. When he picked up his pace, they picked up their pace.

When Evie saw the man enter a restaurant, she expected Tom to suggest stopping for an early luncheon, but he didn't.

Instead of asking, she stated, "You know that man."

Tom gave a distracted nod and murmured, "Yes."

Evie studied him for a moment and tried to read his intentions. Tom appeared to be looking down the street. However, Evie guessed his eyes were slanted toward the restaurant. Also, they had slowed down to a snail's pace.

Tom cupped her elbow and they both stopped and

turned, almost, Evie thought, as if they were discussing whether to continue or turn back.

She followed the prompt without questioning him. Although, she felt compelled to ask, "Shall I just pretend we're having a conversation?" She shifted Holmes, positioning her hand under his chin.

Again, Tom nodded.

"Well, Holmes and I are rather curious to find out what or whom you've noticed but you seem to be captivated by the object of your attention, so we are left to form our very own opinions." Evie hummed for a moment. "Let's see... Oh, yes, I think you've seen someone who might have a questionable past and I can't help but wonder where you might have met this person."

Tom continued to look straight ahead, but his gaze remained slanted and focused on the restaurant. "Questionable past?" he murmured.

"Yes, indeed. If the man had been an ordinary person with an ordinary past, you might have approached him and renewed your acquaintance. Instead, you're keeping a safe distance. That also suggests you don't wish to be recognized by him or betray the fact you are currently watching him."

The edge of Tom's lip lifted. "Countess, your mind is a place of unrelenting activity and boundless curiosity and imagination."

Feeling quite pleased, she said, "I'll take that as a compliment. Here's another theory. This person of interest could be someone from back home." Evie knew she had cast a wide net. Tom had worked as a wildcatter in the Oklahoma oil fields where he had made his fortune. Who knew what type of people he had met there. Could one of them have made his way here to England?

Of course, Tom had also joined the Expeditionary forces during the Great War. The man could be someone he had crossed paths with there. Perhaps an enemy.

She wished he would come out and tell her…

"Countess, I'll tell you in a minute."

"Did you just read my mind?"

"I don't need to. I just know your curiosity is hard at work trying to figure out the identity of the person who has caught my interest but, at the same time, you just wish to know."

"I see. It's not just your attention but your interest as well. That can only mean there is a real mystery about him." She looked down at Holmes and smiled. "I'm sure you'll tell me all about it in due course. Meanwhile, I'll chat with Holmes. He's a great listener and I know he likes to hear me talk because, when I do, he always wags his tail. Unless, of course, you'd prefer it if I simply… shut up?"

"Never," he murmured.

Cupping her elbow again, Tom guided Evie toward a store, positioning himself so he could look at the reflection on the glass window.

"This is exciting. We appear to be playing a game of subterfuge. Are you going to gesture with your hand to express your interest in something?" Evie asked.

"I might just do that," he said. "In fact, I'm about to point at something. You can take over from there."

When he pointed, Evie sighed. "Really, Tom? You like that gown? I don't know how to break this to you, but pink is not really your color. However, that burgundy cloche hat with the light blue flowers would look lovely on you."

Focusing on the reflection she could see on the window, Evie saw the man step out of the restaurant. That surprised her. He'd only been in there for a few minutes.

The man tucked something inside his pocket, looked at his watch and then glanced up and down the street. After another look at his watch, he headed along North Audley Street, in the opposite direction, toward Grosvenor Square. Or, rather, toward Woodridge House.

"Are we following him?" Evie asked.

Tom nodded.

"Well, that's refreshing. The last time we were in town, we were the ones being followed."

They continued on, trailing behind the man at a sedate pace, at one point, almost losing sight of him as he reached a busy street corner.

"I must say, he is well-dressed. He looks quite dapper in his gray suit but the way he has his hat slightly tilted gives him an air of roguishness. I wouldn't be surprised if he has a scar on his cheek."

"He doesn't," Tom murmured.

Evie thought Tom could only know that if he knew him very well.

"He is someone I recognize," Tom finally said. "We crossed paths during the war. I'm afraid I couldn't really tell you what he did."

"Oh, it must have been quite dreadful and secretive."

"No, I mean, I don't actually know what he did. He appeared to be a facilitator of sorts. A man who could make things happen."

"Such as?"

"If one wanted information, he was the man to approach."

"A spy?"

"He might not have defined himself as a spy but he certainly carried out such activities, I'm sure of it."

"Do you think he's involved in something?"

The edge of his lip lifted. "I'd be surprised if he isn't. I'm just curious to see how he is employing his talents during peacetime."

Evie looked up and realized they were about to reach Woodridge House.

Tom must have also noticed because he asked, "Do you wish to stop?"

"Oh, heavens, no. I wouldn't dream of it, not now that I've become invested in learning more."

He cocked an eyebrow at her.

"By that, I mean, I have walked further than you. Therefore, I have put in twice the amount of effort into this pursuit."

"How do you figure that?" he asked.

"Tsk, tsk. Walk a mile in my shoes and you will understand." The heels in her shoes were quite moderate. Nevertheless, they were higher than his regular heels.

Evie glanced at one of the Woodridge House windows just as a curtain shifted. She saw someone appear. A second later, they moved closer, as if focusing on something. Or, rather, someone.

"I believe we have been sighted."

"No, I'm sure he doesn't know we're following him," Tom said.

Evie smiled. "I should clarify. We have been seen by

someone inside Woodridge House." Any minute, she expected the front door to open.

As they drew parallel with the steps leading to the front door, it did indeed open. A footman peered out and then looked over his shoulder as if to convey a message to someone standing behind him. Most likely her butler, Edgar.

"The footman might be trying to determine our intentions. I imagine he is saying we are displaying quite bizarre behavior and walking right past the house. Now I can picture Edgar clucking his tongue and deciding to look for himself. Oh, there he is," she said in a breezy tone. Evie gave her butler a discreet wave. Finding inspiration, she beckoned him over.

Edgar tugged at his sleeve, lifted his chin, and stepped out of the house. He looked to the left and the right and then promptly walked down the steps, approaching them at a businesslike pace.

Evie gestured again, this time suggesting he should maintain a discreet distance. At least, that was her intention. She would only know if he understood her signal by his reaction.

Evie smiled to herself. They really didn't need to take such precautions because the man they had been following walked on ahead at a good distance away from them.

Once Edgar caught up with them, he moved away and put more than an arm's-length between them, his manner businesslike, as if he had trekked out to carry out an errand.

Evie waited for a couple of passersby to walk on by before asking, "Edgar, can you hear me?"

He gave a barely noticeable nod. "Yes, my lady."

"Please ask Edmonds to bring the motor car around and follow us."

Tom glanced at her.

Shrugging, Evie said, "Just in case."

Tom chortled and returned his attention to the man.

"If I may ask, my lady. Are you in danger?"

"No, Edgar. We are merely being discreet."

"Very well, my lady. I shall instruct Edmonds to follow you." Edgar nodded and appeared to notice something on the ground. He stopped and bent down. Straightening, he swung on his heels and returned to Woodridge House.

"Heavens, I shouldn't be surprised at Edgar's acting skills. He is, after all, a theater lover."

A short while later, Evie saw the Duesenberg driving alongside them. She nudged Tom. "We have company. Do you wish to give Edmonds instructions?"

Tom narrowed his gaze. The man continued walking on a straight trajectory and he was a good street block away.

"I think this is as far as we should go." He walked over to have a brief word with Edmonds. After which, he rejoined Evie. "I'm sure luncheon will be ready soon. We wouldn't want to miss that."

Evie could not have looked more surprised. "That's it? You're abandoning the pursuit?"

"Edmonds will follow him and report back." After a moment, Tom added, "I suppose you find it all quite strange."

Evie's brow furrowed. "Following the man? No, not really."

He smiled. "Only you would say that."

They turned back and headed toward Woodridge House.

Tom cleared his throat. "The fact of the matter is, I know he dabbled in clandestine activities. Perhaps he has now put it all behind him."

"And he is now leading an ordinary life?" Evie offered.

"You don't sound convinced," Tom remarked.

Shrugging, Evie said, "I only know what you've told me, which hasn't been much." She drew in a deep breath. "In my opinion, people rarely change. In fact, most people are creatures of habit and stick to what they know. You expressed curiosity about his current activities."

Tom nodded.

"You say you met him during the war, during which time he was involved in questionable activities. Now circumstances have changed. We are living in peaceful times. As you mentioned, you wondered what he is doing now, during peacetime."

"Are you about to say he hasn't strayed far from what he knows?" Tom asked.

Evie gave him a bright smile that reached all the way up to her eyes. "I love it when you follow the thread."

He chortled. "I know what you mean. You find having to explain things unbearably annoying."

"Really? How do you know?"

"Whenever you are called to explain, you have a way of wincing. Oh, it's barely noticeable, but there nonetheless."

Surprised, Evie said, "I hope it's only a wince and not a nervous twitch. I'd hate to have developed one of those. Anyhow, as you said, it is possible he hasn't strayed far from what he knows. That means, you were quite right in wanting to follow him. In any case, Holmes and I found it very entertaining." And now, Evie wondered if Tom wished to take the excursion a step further.

Would he remain curious?

Evie wouldn't be surprised if Edmonds reported back and said he had followed the man to a restaurant where he ate a meal and then made his way to a gentlemen's club to read his newspaper. On any given day, most gentlemen of means did precisely that.

They reached Woodridge House and stopped for a moment to look down the street.

"Tom, during the war, whose side was he on?"

"I believe he was on our side."

That didn't sound very convincing. "Are you suggesting he might have been on the side of whoever dangled the biggest carrot?"

He gave it some thought. "I don't really wish to cast aspersions on his character. However..." He shook his head. "He was just an incredibly difficult character to make out. In fact, if I'd ever given him any thought, I would have pictured him emerging from the shadows and peering around a corner."

The image he created sent a shiver along Evie's spine.

"I really don't know what to think. My interest is probably groundless."

As if in silent agreement, they both walked up the steps with Tom saying, "I'm looking forward to an uneventful luncheon. Although, I'm sure Henrietta will have a tale or two to tell."

Evie laughed. "She'll be too busy interrogating me about the interviews."

CHAPTER 3

Woodridge House
North Audley Street, Mayfair

While freshening up, Evie wondered if she should mention anything about their excursion. If she did, she'd be tempting fate.

She knew Henrietta would ask about the interviews and perhaps express an opinion about the hiring of a lady's maid. Evie wouldn't mind that. However, any mention of their encounter with a mysterious man would intrigue Henrietta who would want to know more, but Tom didn't appear to be inclined to share his knowledge.

Evie decided she wasn't being entirely fair on him. After all, he'd said the man had been difficult to describe, and he hadn't been referring to his demeanor.

Since Tom hadn't said much about the man, Evie was left to form her own conclusions. In her mind, she labeled him the mystery man and mystery men usually skulked about in the shadows, harboring nefarious intentions.

What if he turned out to be dangerous?

She couldn't risk Henrietta and the others becoming involved.

Nodding, Evie decided it would be best not to mention their encounter. At least, not until they knew more.

Henrietta, Sara and Toodles had all come up to town with them, each one saying they had a long list of activities to get through; people to visit, luncheons and dinners to attend and new gowns to acquire.

True to their word, they had all been rather busy. Yet today they had chosen to stay in. She hoped that meant they had thoroughly exhausted themselves and were too fatigued to notice anything unusual.

And then there was Millicent…

Evie had no idea if Edgar had mentioned anything about her strange behavior in the street to Millicent. If he had, Millicent did not refer to it. Her secretary remained preoccupied with the task of employing a new lady's maid. Or, rather, the perfect lady's maid.

She had received a fresh list of candidates and was in the process of selecting the ones she thought worthy of attention.

"Milady, would tomorrow be too soon to set up the interviews?" Millicent asked.

Evie was about to say yes, it would be fine, when she wondered if Tom would be up to the challenge of sitting through another round of interviews.

His interest in the man he had encountered today had been difficult to define and the question remained wide open in her mind. She assumed his mind would be equally engaged.

Evie twirled a hairpin in her hand. Claiming he was merely curious to know what someone he had met during the war was doing now sounded like a reasonable explanation. However, Evie suspected there might be more to Tom's curiosity.

Evie thought about the times she'd encountered someone she didn't expect or want to meet. Usually, she wanted to head in the opposite direction.

What if Tom's surprise at seeing the man in London had been triggered by something else?

Evie tapped the hairpin on the dressing table.

If Tom had assumed the man had been dead...

She nodded. Yes, that would justify his surprise.

She imagined Tom thinking the man had suffered a different fate, one which prevented him from walking around, enjoying his freedom.

"Aha!" she exclaimed.

"Milady?"

Evie turned. "Sorry, did you say something?"

"The interviews... Would tomorrow be too soon?" Millicent asked.

"Oh... I'm not sure about tomorrow, Millicent. Try to schedule the appointments for the next day, please. Actually, next week. Yes, I think next week will be more convenient."

Millicent made a note of Evie's request and, setting her notebook down, she said, "I've been thinking it might be a good idea to set up a second interview. That is, once you decide on at least two candidates."

"A second interview? Whatever for?"

"To be sure, milady."

They were already putting the candidates through the wringer. What else did Millicent have in mind?

"It would be a practical interview," Millicent explained. "The prospective lady's maid could come in for a couple of hours, perhaps as you get ready for an outing. We could let her decide what you should wear. That will give us a clear indication of her tastes."

Evie looked at the wardrobe. Sometimes, she wondered if she had ever had a say in what she wore. In the past, Caro had always made the final decisions and Evie had been happy to indulge her. Now Millicent took care of her wardrobe and made all decisions. On a few rare occasions, Evie pushed herself to express her preferences. However, more often than not, she found herself preoccupied with one thing or another and only too happy to let her maid decide.

Millicent continued, "To make it more interesting, you should criticize her choices."

"Criticize? Why?"

"To see how she takes criticism, of course. There's no point in going to the trouble of holding a second interview if we don't bother getting as much information as we can. She might have an explosive temperament. It would be best to find out before we make any commitments."

Evie wanted to say it all sounded like nonsense but then she'd risk sounding like... Toodles or Henrietta. Or even Sara.

Then she realized Millicent was only being her creative self, a trait Evie wished to find in the new lady's maid.

Or did she?

Perhaps it was enough to have one creative person in her immediate orbit.

Doing her best to sound diplomatic, Evie said, "That sounds like a solid plan, Millicent. However, I don't wish to raise someone's hopes only to then dash them. I will simply select the best candidate from the interviews." She stood up and walked to the door. "Actually, we might want to avoid hiring someone who is merely after a new position. I'd rather employ someone who really needs the job."

Millicent smiled and looked down at the floor for a moment. "You seem to forget, milady, lady's maids are rather scarce at the moment."

"Really? But I've already interviewed six of them."

Millicent nodded. "They all have positions and their experience makes them quite sought after."

She was in competition with other women looking to employ a new lady's maid?

Evie gave a nod of understanding. They were all looking for a change. Well, they would certainly find it here…

Sighing, she said, "We can forget about Merrin Smith. She doesn't like foreigners."

Millicent nodded. "I've already crossed her off the list. Remember, I showed you Lotte Mannering's report."

Evie left it at that and made her way downstairs where she found Tom sitting in the hall.

"Why haven't you gone in? Millicent said the others were already in the dining room."

Tom set his newspaper down and stood up. "I thought

I would have another read of the newspaper, just in case I missed something."

"What do you think you might have missed?"

"I'm not sure." He shrugged. "I won't know until I find it."

Hearing the uncertainty in Tom's voice worried Evie. Had seeing that man today rattled his nerves?

"Were you trying to find a reason for the man's presence in Mayfair? Perhaps some sort of clandestine goings on?"

He nodded and, after a measured moment, said, "Yes, I think I was…"

Evie looked toward the front door. "I take it Edmonds hasn't returned."

Tom shook his head. "No, and that's another reason why I've been sitting here. There's also a third reason." He lightened the mood by grinning. "I was waiting for you."

"Does that worry you?" Evie rolled her eyes. "I mean… that Edmonds hasn't returned yet."

"I'll try not to let it worry me. It's only been fifty-three minutes."

Heavens. He'd been keeping track, right down to the minute. "Tom, please tell me that man is not dangerous."

"Oh, no. It's the oddest thing. I never saw him carrying a weapon."

"Well, that's a relief." Or was it? What if the man employed other methods to dispose of people?

Suddenly, Evie found herself entertaining images of hidden knives or poison, or even a gang of assassins under his command…

They headed for the dining room and walked in just as

Henrietta, the Dowager Countess of Woodridge said, "Evangeline doesn't pander to critics."

Toodles, Evie's granny, smiled. "No, indeed. She never has. In fact, she refers to critics as petty annoyances. That doesn't mean she considers herself above reproach. She only thinks critics ought to look at themselves in the mirror before casting aspersions."

Heavens, what had she walked into and why were they discussing her?

"Oh, here she is," Henrietta exclaimed. "Would you care to explain yourself, Evangeline?"

Evie took her place at the table and wished Tom hadn't decided to sit across from her. "I'm not sure that I do, Henrietta. Am I being accused of something?"

Sara, her mother in law, gave her a brisk smile. "Henrietta has been describing you to us. She feels opinions vary and she wished to know how we perceived you."

"Why?"

Sara looked at Henrietta before saying, "I'm not sure. I believe she was rattling off a few ideas to kill time while we waited for you and Tom. A moment before she made that statement, we were talking about manners and wondering if they were going out of fashion. Yes, I believe that's when she changed the subject and made you the focus of her attention."

Sighing, Henrietta explained, "As Sara said a moment ago, opinions vary. There is only one of you but I might think of you in one way and Sara might have a different opinion of you and so on and so forth."

A quick glance at Tom assured Evie she wasn't the only one confounded by the conversation. "I believe Tom and I should make a point of entering a room right at the start of a conversation."

Edgar cleared his throat, drawing everyone's attention to him.

He stood by the door. When they all turned, he proceeded to announce, "Lady Evans."

"Caro?" Had she lost track of time? Lady Evans wasn't expected for another two days.

"And that," Tom said, "is another way of changing the subject and sparing you the ordeal of explaining yourself."

Evie pressed her hand to her eye.

Good heavens. Had she twitched?

Caro walked in, her steps tentative. "I'm ever so sorry to barge in unexpectedly."

Evie didn't have to ask Edgar to set another place at the table. He had already signaled the footmen who were busy setting up a place next to Sara.

"I suppose there is no point in arguing against joining you for luncheon." Caro sat down. She must have sensed everyone at the table looking at her. Shrugging, she said, "I made a last-minute decision to come to town earlier than planned and... I suppose I should have telephoned ahead."

"Nonsense," Henrietta offered. "I know I speak for everyone. You are always welcomed here."

Caro arranged a napkin on her lap. "I wasn't even sure if you would be at home."

Henrietta gave her an impish smile. "Evangeline is interviewing for a new lady's maid. Personally, I cannot wait to see how it all turns out. Although, after our experience with her last attempt to find a secretary, I wouldn't be surprised if we are all murdered in our sleep."

Caro nodded but she appeared to be lost in her own thoughts, something Evie found odd because, when Caro had been her lady's maid, she'd always had a lot to say. Indeed, Evie knew she'd have firm opinions about the hiring of the right person.

"Henrietta, rest assured, I will make a point of engaging someone incapable of committing murder. Millicent is being quite thorough and leaving no stone unturned."

Again, Evie expected Caro to say something but Caro was now enthralled by the intricate design on the plate.

Evie glanced at Tom. Earlier, he had looked forward to enjoying an uneventful luncheon. So far, they had walked right into the middle of a conversation which had promised or, rather, threatened to force Evie into defending herself and then, Caro had paid them a surprise visit.

Tom, who usually responded to her glances, was preoccupied with studying the design of his own plate. If she had to guess, she'd say Tom's mind continued to be engaged on the man he had seen on the street.

That reminded Evie she hadn't even asked the man's name.

As Evie took a bite of her entrée, she glanced at Caro.

Apart from her greeting and opening remark, she hadn't said anything about her reasons for coming to town early.

She saw Henrietta exchange a look with Toodles which suggested she had noticed something. When Henrietta looked at Caro her eyebrows rose a fraction.

Something had clearly caught Henrietta's attention.

Perhaps nothing more than Caro's silence.

When Caro had been her lady's maid, she had been quite a chatterbox, never afraid to express her opinions or fleeting thoughts. Now that she'd become Lady Evans, her mannerisms were more reserved but that didn't stop her from expressing herself.

Evie watched Caro pushing around a potato. "Caro, will Henry be joining you?"

Startled, Caro speared the potato and delivered it to her mouth. It seemed the small morsel required a great deal of chewing, so she offered a small shake of her head, followed by a shrug and several gestures which Evie couldn't quite interpret.

So…

Henry was either not coming or she didn't actually know.

"Oh, of course," Sara exclaimed. "You must have come up early to prepare for the presentation."

"What presentation?" Tom asked.

"That's not for another month or so," Henrietta interjected. "Do you have your gown ready?"

Caro speared another potato and lifted the fork to her mouth at the same time as she nodded.

Tom cast his gaze around the table. Finally, he fixed his attention on Evie, his eyebrow lifted. It took her a moment to remember his question as well as the answer. "Oh, it's *the* presentation."

"I'm still in the dark," he admitted.

In the dark and eager to distract himself, Evie thought.

"As the new Lady Evans, Caro will be presented to the King and Queen," Henrietta explained.

"I thought that was only reserved for debutantes," Toodles said.

"Not at all," Sara replied and glanced at Tom. "In fact…"

Henrietta shot her a warning look.

Evie had no trouble interpreting the warning. If Henrietta succeeded in gaining a title for Tom, he would attend the function and, he would be required to wear knee breeches.

"I remember my presentation," Sara mused. "Henrietta forced me to spend an hour a day for an entire week walking up and down the long gallery with a book balanced on my head. Back then, she still rode and she always made sure the exercise took place directly before her morning ride so she could appear dressed in her riding clothes and her riding crop in hand."

Henrietta did not deny this. Instead, she looked quite pleased with herself.

"Did she threaten you with it?" Toodles asked.

"She tapped the riding crop against her thigh in tune with the metronome, something else she insisted I use. Now that I think about it, Henrietta was quite diabolical. I had nightmares about missing a step."

Darting a glance at the clock on the mantle, Tom returned his attention to his meal and resumed his silent introspection.

If Edmonds didn't return soon, Evie imagined Tom would take up pacing or send out a search party.

But where would they start looking?

Evie fell into her own silent introspection.

When the footmen removed the main course plates and served the dessert, Evie found herself glancing at the clock.

Conversation flowed around her. The others had definitely noticed her silence, but they did not question it.

Yes, they were definitely curious…

Evie sensed their glances traveling around the table, bouncing between Tom and Caro and Evie.

Just as well Caro had been a late arrival, otherwise, Evie imagined, Henrietta would be weaving a tale of conspiracy between the three silent diners.

Evie found herself pondering the idea of conspiracies, for no other reason other than to keep her mind busy and away from watching the clock on the mantle.

"Edgar," Henrietta said, "please send our compliments to the cook. It was a splendid meal, not that Evangeline, Tom or even Caro noticed."

CHAPTER 4

*E*vie snapped out of her quiet introspection and looked up. "Oh, yes. Luncheon was delicious." She had no idea how she had managed to get through the meal without biting her tongue or choking.

Between thinking about Caro's silence and early arrival and wondering if there was any significance to Tom's encounter that morning, she hadn't been able to settle down to enjoy the meal.

Henrietta shared a look with Sara and Toodles which conveyed some sort of communication, confirmed by the fact they all nodded. Turning back to Evie, she said, "Evangeline, I should like to enjoy a cup of coffee now."

It took a moment for Henrietta's remark to register in Evie's mind. "Oh, yes. That would be lovely."

Again, Henrietta looked at the others, this time her expression looked puzzled. Sara and Toodles looked equally mystified.

Henrietta gave the door a pointed look and then

turned to Evie, something Evie found strange, only to belatedly realize they were all waiting for her to make a move.

Evie shot to her feet. "Shall we?"

Smiling, Henrietta nodded, "Yes, of course."

Evie had never questioned the customs and traditions of English society. Right from the start, she'd known she was marrying into a family with an established history. They adhered to certain rules and ways of doing things and it wasn't her place to question them.

As petty as they might appear to some, the rules of precedence were observed, even at a casual luncheon at home. As the Countess of Woodridge, it was her place to lead them out of the dining room.

Evie headed for the drawing room where she seated herself on the sofa, inviting Caro to sit beside her. Never mind that she would have preferred to remain behind to have a private word with Tom.

He had joined them and continued to look preoccupied, standing by the fireplace, his hand resting on the mantle, his fingers drumming a silent tune.

Edgar walked in, followed by a footman carrying a tray with coffee.

As the footman set the tray on a table, Edgar cleared his throat and announced, "Edmonds has returned and wishes to speak with Mr. Winchester."

Evie surged to her feet but remained standing in place while Tom nearly tripped over the furniture trying to get to the door.

Instead of following him out, Edgar stood by the door… the open door.

From where she stood, Evie could see Edmonds standing at the far end of the hall. Out of the corner of her eye, she also saw Henrietta exchange a raised eyebrow look with Sara and Toodles.

Evie expected Henrietta to demand a full account of the morning's activities because, surely, something had happened and they were now witnessing some sort of development but, to her surprise, she did not ask for an explanation.

Returning her focus to Tom and Edmonds, Evie stifled a soft growl filled with frustration. She could only see Tom's back so she couldn't read his expression, and his body language did not give anything away.

Heavens, he didn't even nod his head.

Edmonds, on the other hand, stood facing her. As he spoke, he shook his head, nodded and gestured with his hands. Evie searched for signs that he might have run into some sort of trouble but she found none.

Tom's stillness had her tensing with anticipation. What could they possibly be talking about?

Suddenly, Evie gasped. She only then realized she had been feeling quite anxious about Edmonds' wellbeing.

If something had happened to him, she would never have forgiven herself. After all, she had been responsible for sending him on a fool's errand.

Unable to bear the suspense, Evie excused herself and walked out of the drawing room, her heels clicking on the wooden floor.

When she reached Tom and Edmonds, they both looked at her.

She felt compelled to apologize for interrupting and explained, "Whatever has happened, I would prefer it if we didn't involve the others. Henrietta is eager for some entertainment and I don't wish whatever this is to turn into a circus."

"Edmonds was just saying he followed Wilfred Greer—"

"Oh, so that's his name."

Tom nodded. "He had lunch at The Red Lion."

Evie recognized the name. "The pub in St James's?"

"Yes. He met a young woman and Edmonds says she handed him an envelope. She did not join him for a meal."

So the woman's purpose must have been to deliver... something. Evie remembered the man... Wilfred Greer, putting something in his coat pocket when he'd exited the restaurant. It had looked like an envelope and that would make it the second envelope he'd collected that morning. Or, rather, the first.

Was that his purpose in being here, in London? To collect envelopes. What did they contain?

Tom continued, "Then, Wilfred Greer went to White's."

Evie drew a map of the area in her mind and placed the pub and the gentlemen's club. Drawing a line between the two, she followed Wilfred Greer's trajectory.

"Edmonds was just saying he might still be there. He couldn't follow him inside..." Tom brushed his hand across his chin.

Of course, being a private gentlemen's club, one would either have to be a member or know someone who would invite him in as a guest. Evie studied Tom and suspected he might be trying to decide if he should take further action.

If he went to White's, he'd risk being seen by the man. "Lotte Mannering," she suggested without hesitation.

Tom looked at her. "At such short notice?"

His quick response made Evie smile. He hadn't asked for an explanation because he'd understood her meaning.

"If she doesn't go there herself, albeit disguised as a man, she'll know whom to contact. In fact, I wouldn't be surprised if she knows someone who works at the club." She signaled to the library. "You should hurry."

Without further delay, Tom headed for the library to make the telephone call while Evie thanked Edmonds and returned to the drawing room.

As she walked in, she felt all eyes pinned on her but, once again, no one asked her to explain herself.

Just in case they tried to prod, Evie proceeded to ask Caro about everyone she and Tom had met during their last visit, including Caro's colorful mother-in-law. "Caro, I must apologize. I simply forgot to ask earlier. My mind has been dulled by the interviews I held this morning."

Caro's brief responses left too many gaps and Evie feared Henrietta would interrupt with a pointed question about the conversation she'd had in the hall with Edmonds and Tom.

"We should visit you again soon," Evie chirped. "I'm sure by now Tom has forgotten about Lady Louisa wanting to paint him. Will she be joining you in town?"

"I'm… not sure. It's not the sort of affair she enjoys."

"Yes, of course. I'd forgotten." Despite being a titled lady, Caro's mother-in-law avoided grand social events in favor of the quiet life she enjoyed in the country with her chickens and her art.

Risking a glance at Henrietta and the others, Evie saw they were all drinking their coffee while watching her and continuing to exchange glances that spoke of increasing curiosity.

Any minute now, Evie expected them to burst into a barrage of questions. Surely, it was bound to happen.

Determined to keep the situation contained, Evie walked to the table and helped herself to a cup of coffee, stirring in one lump of sugar as she asked if Caro had found any secret passages in her house. Caro had now been living there as the new Lady Evans for a number of months and would have had many opportunities to explore the large house. But, again, Caro responded with a brisk shake of her head.

Evie couldn't explain Caro's uncharacteristic behavior, especially as she had no room in her mind as it continued to focus on that morning's strange activities.

Returning to the sofa, Evie took a sip of coffee just as Tom entered the drawing room and sat down near the fireplace. He appeared to be more relaxed so Evie assumed he had succeeded in contacting Lotte Mannering and engaging her services, picking up where Edmonds had left off at White's.

Forcing herself to believe everything had somehow been sorted out, she turned to Caro. However, she'd run out of conversation. To her dismay, Caro remained silent and Henrietta and the others appeared to be quite content just observing.

She couldn't rely on Tom to bail her out. At least his silence could be excused—he simply had a lot on his mind. On the other hand, Henrietta's silence could not be explained. She always had something to say and, while Evie didn't want her asking the sort of questions that would force her to reveal their activities, she needed someone to break the silence.

Caro's lip quivered as she startled everyone by declaring, "I've... *I've left Henry.*"

Evie's cup rattled on its saucer. "What?"

Caro gave a stiff nod. "I have walked out on Henry." Her cheeks flashed a deep shade of crimson. Her voice was a mixture of determination and anxiety.

Sara shifted to the edge of her seat. "Caro? What happened?"

Caro's lip quivered. "He was positively beastly. I thought I'd married a gentleman and he turned into... into... into *a beast.*"

Henrietta's eyes widened. "My dear, what did he do?"

Caro gave a fierce shake of her head. "It's too awful to say. He... He asked me to do something... and he made it impossible for me to say no and then... and then I caught the train and that's when I decided I would leave him. Or maybe I made the decision the moment I walked out the door. Perhaps even when I grabbed my coat and handbag."

Henrietta gasped. Toodles shook her head in disbelief and Sara merely blinked.

Tom snapped out of his reverie and shot to his feet. His jaws clenched and his eyes narrowed to slits.

Reading his intentions, Evie said, "Tom. Do please sit down."

"Yes, Tom," Henrietta urged. "There is a penalty for murder and I can read the intention in your eyes."

A moment of confusion followed then Caro gasped. "Oh." Caro looked from one to the other. "Henry doesn't deserve such a harsh penalty but he could do with a good horse whipping."

Tom nodded, buttoned his coat and made a move to leave.

"Tom," Evie urged. "*He is a policeman.*"

"Perhaps it might be best if Tom left the room," Toodles suggested. "Then Caro can confide in us and give us all the gruesome details."

"Oh, that's not necessary." Caro gave a fierce shake of her head and declared, "I want the whole world to know what a horrible person I married." She released her hold on her posture and slumped. "Now I will be plain Caro again."

Smiling, Henrietta assured her, "Oh, no dear. You get to keep the title. And we will help you find the best legal counsel to represent you. Divorce is becoming quite fashionable." Henrietta tilted her head. "Do you wish to proceed with or without a scandal? Scandals make it much more interesting. Once upon a time, the news would have been whispered in drawing rooms." Henrietta's eyes brightened. "Now we have the broadsheets divulging the most unsavory and salacious secrets. It's all quite entertaining. Just what we need."

One by one, everyone sitting in the drawing room looked at her and blinked in disbelief.

Evie couldn't even begin to imagine what Lord Evans had wanted Caro to do. Of course, the doors would be open to her. She could return to Halton House with them and remain for as long as she wanted or needed to.

While she couldn't picture Lord Evans behaving in a beastly manner, she didn't feel right forcing Caro to share details.

Thankfully, the others did not offer any unnecessary platitudes to encourage Caro to open up.

Caro seemed determined to stand her ground. She gave a fierce shake of her head. "No. I can't ever go back."

Henrietta caught Edgar's attention. "Some tea, please, Edgar. Very strong and very sweet."

Evie felt at a loss. She'd never had a single disagreement with her husband. She imagined words spoken in haste would make any situation look more dismal than it actually was.

"What exactly did Lord Evans demand of you, Caro?" Henrietta asked.

Evie gasped. "Henrietta, perhaps this isn't the time—"

"Oh, my dear, there is never a perfect time for such things. Although, right now would be ideal. Get it all out in the open and then we'll find a solution and move on."

Caro stared at Henrietta for a moment, her eyes wide, her cheeks flushed.

Evie couldn't tell if she felt distraught by the prospect of talking about her experience or if she couldn't believe what Henrietta had just proposed.

Sara nudged Henrietta. In response, Henrietta said, "It's only a suggestion."

Caro turned to Evie and hiccupped.

Evie pressed her hand on Caro's hand and gave it a squeeze. "Caro, you don't need to tell anyone."

Caro stilled and held Evie's gaze. Giving a firm nod, she appeared to reach a decision. When she spoke, her words spilled out with purpose. "Henry has forbidden me to have anything to do with your investigations. He's only concerned about his reputation and how it might look if my photograph is plastered all over the newspapers because that's where I'll end up, of course."

The room fell silent as everyone appeared to process the information and dismiss everything else they had obviously been imagining.

Henrietta was the first to find her voice, "But why would he think that?"

"Because he knows me only too well and says I will stop at nothing and my wild ideas will be the end of me or him, I'm not sure which. At that point, he really wasn't making much sense. Or, rather, I couldn't understand what he was saying because I'd become enraged and I grabbed my handbag and coat and left him."

Everyone eased back in their seats, their expressions not as surprised as Evie would have liked.

Indeed, Henrietta's eyes filled with mirth, while Sara and Toodles lifted their cups of coffee to hide their smiles.

Sounding astonished, Evie said, "I'm not sure why everyone finds this so amusing."

"Evangeline, you're a bad influence. If I recall, at least two of us have appeared in the front page of the newspapers being hauled away by the police. If not for you, we would never have been anywhere near that den of iniquity."

Evie's lips parted. "Den of iniquity? I think you might be suffering from a case of foggy memory."

Henrietta lifted her chin and declared, "I have the newspaper clipping to prove it."

"You kept a souvenir?"

"Of course. Someday, I might wish to write my memoirs."

The doors opened and Edgar walked in carrying the tea Henrietta had asked for as well as the afternoon edition of the newspaper.

Eager to take advantage of the interruption, Evie walked over to the table, poured a cup of tea for Caro and handed it to her. Glancing at Tom, she wondered what he'd made of all this. His expression failed to reveal the inner workings of his mind which, in itself, might actually suggest he had turned his thoughts elsewhere.

Lord Evans' request struck Evie as odd. When they'd visited Caro, she had only recently returned from her honeymoon. Evie remembered Caro saying that as a detective's wife she didn't wish to do anything that would then reflect badly on her husband because if he ever heard any of his colleagues talking about her meddling in matters that shouldn't concern her, he would most likely roll up his sleeves and give them a black eye.

Taking a sip of her sweet tea, Caro looked up and smiled. "Thank you. This is just what I needed."

"Evangeline," Henrietta said, "this might be a good moment for you to offer Caro a firm assurance. As her friend, you must tell her there is absolutely no risk of her becoming involved in an investigation. Not today and not tomorrow or even for the duration of her stay."

Tom shifted so he could look at her. A quick glance at him told Evie he was most keen to hear her assurance.

Turning, Evie walked over to the table to pour herself a cup of tea. "Of course, that goes without saying," she said as she glanced at the newspaper.

Frowning, she set her cup down and picked up the newspaper.

Skimming through the article which had caught her attention she gasped and swung toward Tom.

Merrin Smith...

Arrested for murder.

CHAPTER 5

And when my little baby smiles at me
There's such a wonderful light that shines in her eyes

Ted Lewis & His Band

The library

As soon as Henrietta and the others excused themselves and left to prepare for an evening outing, Evie rushed out of the drawing room and headed for the library. Looking over her shoulder, she eased the door open and hurried inside. "Heavens, I thought they'd never leave."

She found Tom crouched down by the fireplace singing a popular song, something she knew he sometimes did to distract himself.

Setting the fire poker down, he straightened. "My

apologies for bailing out on you, Countess. There's only so much tea and coffee I could drink while being scrutinized by Henrietta, Sara and Toodles."

While his brows were no longer furrowed, he still looked preoccupied with the day's events.

"I'm glad you noticed. I thought I was imagining it all. And then, there's the business with Caro. To be perfectly honest, I don't know what to make of that situation. I'm only glad Caro decided she needed some time alone. She's retired to her room for a lie-down." Evie felt compelled to add, "And I don't feel it's our place to interfere. I'm sure it will soon be sorted out."

"Of course." Tom nodded in agreement. "I hope you realize Henrietta and the others are onto you."

"Yes, absolutely. They know something's happened but, for some reason, they refuse to ask. Just as well because I have no idea what I would say."

She looked down at the newspaper she held. Rushing to the library, she'd debated whether to first ask about his conversation with Lotte Mannering or if she should tell him about the headline. They were both equally important. However, the headline was, by far, the most surprising.

She held the newspaper up. "I've been biting my tongue for a whole hour. I tried to signal you but you were busy with your own thoughts."

"What is it?" he asked. Reading the headline from across the room, his eyebrows curved up. "Is it meant to mean something?"

Evie frowned and looked at the newspaper. "Oh, it's upside down and… I suppose you can't read the fine print from there." Walking up to him, she handed him the newspaper and sat down on the edge of a chair.

"Merrin Smith. Arrested for Murder?" he read.

Evie gave a vigorous nod. "I assume the headline is an exaggeration. The police never charge someone so quickly. Well, not unless they catch someone in the act or holding the weapon…"

Tom read the brief article. "She has been arrested and is being questioned."

Shaking her head, Evie complained, "I can't understand why reporters always do that. Arrested for murder is in large, bold print. If you read the first paragraph, you learn she is being questioned and it's only when you get to the end that you realize the police are still investigating. That can only mean they don't have any physical evidence of wrongdoing but they obviously have something significant enough to hold her for questioning."

Easing down onto a chair opposite Evie, Tom brushed his hand across his chin as he mused, "Yes, I see what you mean. Although, it would have been more dramatic if they had started with *Hangman's noose around woman's neck.*"

"Tom, this is not the time to jest." In the next breath, she added, "Oh, I suppose one must find humor even in irony or sarcasm as a way to remain sane."

"Wait a minute… This is the young woman you interviewed today."

Evie nodded. "Merrin is an unusual name. I can't imagine there being two women named Merrin Smith. It can't be a coincidence."

Tom skimmed through the article again. "There's no mention of a detective's name so I assume the police didn't make a statement. How did the reporters even get her name?"

"That is a very good question." Sitting back, Evie crossed her legs and nibbled the tip of her thumb. "I'm curious about the sequence of events. I interviewed her just before midday." She glanced up at the clock. "It's now five in the afternoon and I saw that article an hour ago. The newspaper must have been rushed out."

He set the newspaper down and looked at Evie. "What do you propose doing about this? I imagine you want to do something…"

"Don't you find it strange? Of all the people who could have committed murder today, it had to be the woman I interviewed."

Tom studied her for a moment and then smiled. "You sound inconvenienced."

"That wasn't my intention and I do wish people would stop misreading me. It's annoying. There, I've said it."

"So what else am I getting wrong about you?"

"I'll grant you a tiny concession because your mind is engaged on other matters. I want answers and the only way to get them will be to contact someone who knows what's happening."

Tom's eyes brightened. "But you promised, Countess. No investigations."

She wanted to correct him and say she had only promised to keep Caro out of an investigation, but decided against it, mostly because she felt rather raw about Henry's opinion of her.

Evie huffed out a breath. Closing her eyes for a moment, she brought to mind the times Henrietta and the others had somehow ended up in the thick of it. Now there was the business with Lord Evans laying down the law.

Yes, whatever happened next, they would have to navigate their way around it all with extreme caution, keeping everyone else out of it and, if pushed for information, they would have to... *lie*.

She closed her eyes and wondered how she could possibly feel so thoroughly exhausted.

A log shifted in the fire. She sensed Tom sitting opposite her. Smiling, she savored the moment and allowed herself to sink into a state of complete relaxation. Telling herself everything in her world would settle back into place, she opened her eyes and was about to finally ask Tom about Lotte Mannering when the library door opened and Edgar walked in.

"I believe we are about to be surprised," Tom murmured.

Edgar forgot to clear his throat. Instead, he looked at Evie and then at the door. Almost as if he couldn't quite believe his eyes. "My lady..."

"Yes, Edgar? What is it?"

"Lord Evans to see you, my lady."

Lord Evans?

Not Detective Inspector Evans?

He usually worked out of Scotland Yard but Caro's husband had clearly not come here on an official capacity.

Good heavens. Had he come here to drag Caro back home? Of course, this would be the first place he'd look for her.

She glanced at Tom. Earlier, he had been prepared to do Caro's bidding and give Lord Evans a good thrashing. Now, he merely smiled, no doubt, finding amusement in the idea of Henry trekking up to London to reclaim his runaway wife.

Lord Evans walked in, his steps confident and businesslike. At least, until he reached the middle of the library. Then, he hesitated. Clearing his throat, he inclined his head. "Lady Woodridge. Mr. Winchester."

Frowning at his formal tone, Evie chirped, "Lord Evans, how lovely to see you."

He looked over his shoulder at Edgar who remained standing by the door.

"My lady, I wonder if I might have a private word with you."

Exchanging a glance with Tom, Evie wondered if he meant to exclude Tom. She didn't think so. Turning to Edgar, she said, "Thank you, Edgar." Although, she had half a mind to ask that he bring in some tea, just in case they needed the interruption.

Her butler nodded and exited the library, no doubt hurrying off to warn Caro of her husband's presence.

Gesturing to a chair, Evie invited him to sit. "Oh, and do please remember to call me Evie." Suddenly, a veil lifted in her mind and Evie remembered Lord Evans… Henry had accused her of being a bad influence. He had quite possibly accused her of a great many other infractions but Caro had either been too upset or uncharacteristically diplomatic and hadn't mentioned them.

"I'm actually here on an official capacity."

That took Evie by surprise.

He glanced at the newspaper Tom had set aside and shook his head.

Exchanging a knowing glance with Tom, Evie asked,

"Does your business, by any chance, have anything to do with Merrin Smith?"

"Yes, indeed. Her name was not supposed to appear in the newspaper, but that's another matter."

Evie assumed someone had made some extra cash on the side, delivering the tidbit to a reporter, something the police would frown upon.

Detective Inspector Evans did not beat about the bush. "Merrin Smith claims to know you."

"We met this morning," Evie admitted. Sitting back, she realized the detective didn't quite look like his usual self. In fact, he looked slightly rumpled, but not in an obvious way. From the first moment of meeting him some time ago, Evie had noticed his tidy appearance. His gray suit looked freshly pressed and his striped blue and gold tie had a perfect knot. Yet, there appeared to be something slightly disheveled about him, but she couldn't quite put her finger on it.

"Could you describe your meeting with her, please?" the detective asked.

Evie could very easily imagine Tom saying it had been a torturous test in patience for Merrin Smith.

"I'm in the process of hiring a lady's maid," Evie explained. In her mind, Evie heard Tom snort so she gave him a warning frown to which he replied with a slight lift of his shoulders and eyebrows.

She was about to say more about her encounter when the detective asked, "Did she mention her employer by name?"

Evie searched her mind. "I don't think she did. Is that important?"

The detective looked at Tom. "Were you present at the interview?"

"Not really. I sat a short distance away."

"Could you hear the conversation?"

"To be perfectly honest, I was barely aware of the interview taking place. I was reading the newspaper." Tom turned to Evie. "Didn't you take notes?"

"No. I had a notebook but I used it to remind myself of the questions I had to ask."

"What's this about, Henry?" Tom asked.

That had been the same question swimming in Evie's mind. Along with one other pertinent question. Why hadn't Henry asked about Caro? He had to know she had come to Woodridge House. After all, he was expected to come within a few days…

The detective gestured to the newspaper. "As the article suggests, we are currently questioning Miss Smith but she is being less than cooperative."

"She gave you my name," Evie said.

The detective nodded. "That was her attempt to secure an alibi."

That surprised Evie. "Is that what she said?"

"Not in so many words. We simply assumed—" The detective stopped and rubbed his fingers along his temple.

Evie realized he had caught himself uttering what most would think of as an oversight.

One never simply assumed.

The detective continued, "Can you remember what time the interview ended?"

Evie turned to Tom. When the interview had ended, they had both been thoroughly involved in their lengthy conversation and had lost track of time. Tom's blank expression suggested he couldn't help her out.

"Not with any precision," she finally said. "It was around midday." Evie nodded. "I remember a couple of gentlemen came into the pub. That's where we held the interview."

To Evie's dismay, the detective's expression suggested he found the idea of carrying out such an activity in a pub ludicrous. To her even greater dismay, he was probably justifying warning Caro away from Evie's orbit.

While she didn't wish to tread over invisible lines drawn between her and the official investigation, Evie felt the need to stand her ground. Lifting her chin, she asked, "Who is the person she's been accused of killing?"

"Miss Smith has not been formally charged," he replied.

Evie's eyes widened slightly. She had asked a direct question and, if he didn't answer, she would have to accept his authority.

A log shifted in the fire. Embers sparkled around it and then flew up the chimney.

During that brief pause, Evie wondered if Henry remained focused on the case or if he'd allowed thoughts of his wife to intrude.

The breath he drew in made a soft hissing sound. Relenting, he said, "Mrs. Colliers."

Softening her voice, Evie asked, "And where did Mrs. Colliers reside?" While Evie asked the question, she knew he wouldn't feel obliged to answer. He'd already said too much. Then again, he understood her curiosity came from a need to make sense of a puzzle.

"Why do you ask?"

Evie sat back and drummed her fingers on the armrest. "Merrin Smith told you she met me for an interview. I assume she gave you the location of that interview. In case she didn't, it was at The Marlborough Head in Mayfair, not far from here. As you suggested, she might be trying to establish an alibi. In which case, she mentioned me because she wanted to place herself far away from the scene of the crime. Of course, I'm jumping to conclusions. For all I know, the crime was committed around the corner."

He took a moment to digest what she'd told him.

"Yes, of course," he said under his breath. "Mrs. Colliers lived in Lyall Street, Belgravia. Near Eaton Square." He drew out a small notebook and gave her the precise address.

Evie closed her eyes and tried to place the address. One could walk that distance or catch a taxi-cab.

"Given the right traffic conditions," the detective said, "she could have traveled from the pub to that address within a short time."

That could only mean…

"I take it Mrs. Colliers died shortly after midday or… thereabouts?"

He gave a noncommittal nod.

"How did Miss Smith come to be arrested?" For a moment, Evie thought she had exhausted the concessions the detective had been willing to grant her and she wouldn't receive an answer.

However, he surprised her by revealing the sequence of events in great detail.

"Miss Smith was walking along Lyall Street, heading away from Mrs. Colliers' house. The maid who raised the alarm and placed the telephone call to the police described her. As the police rushed to the scene, they spotted Miss Smith."

Most of the houses in that area were painted white. Anyone walking along would stand out.

"How convenient," she remarked as she wondered what Merrin Smith had been doing in that part of town. "Perhaps she works in the area and had been making her way home."

He tapped a finger on the armrest. "She refuses to give her address."

"Why on earth would she do that?" Even as she asked the question, Evie knew Merrin Smith had to be covering for someone.

"What can you tell me about her behavior during the interview?" the detective asked.

Evie willed herself not to look at Tom. On the one hand, she wished to help with the investigation. However, on the other hand, she wanted to avoid saying anything which might cast a shadow over Merrin Smith's character or reinforce any suspicion the detective might be harboring.

Her observations were based on a brief interview. Merrin had fidgeted and she hadn't been at ease, but Evie took full responsibility for that.

However...

What if Merrin Smith's behavior had reflected her anxiety, not over the interview but rather over what she had planned on doing later on?

Evie looked at Detective Inspector Evans...Lord Evans... Henry... At that moment, she failed to separate one from the other. He had a job to do but, at the same time, he was a titled gentleman and a friend of the family.

Evie shrugged. "Everyone I've interviewed has displayed some sort of uneasiness. That's to be expected."

He studied her for a moment and Evie knew he had to be wondering if she was somehow biased and withholding vital information.

"Did she look more uneasy or less uneasy than the other candidates?"

"I'm afraid I'm entirely responsible for making her uneasy." To Evie's annoyance, the detective did not look surprised. "That's why I find it difficult to give you a straight answer." She glanced at Tom. "You suggested she might have been attending the interview behind her employer's back. It's possible that could have set her on edge."

Tom nodded in agreement.

"Tom, why did you say that?" the detective asked.

Instead of answering, Tom deferred to Evie.

"As a matter of fact, we happened to be discussing her uneasiness." Evie drew in a breath and looked up at the ceiling. Gathering her thoughts, she said, "In answer to your question, she looked more uneasy than the other candidate."

The detective pushed her for more detailed information, asking one question after another until Evie put her hand up. "I realize you are trying to determine her state of mind before she supposedly committed this crime, but there are circumstances which need to be taken into account."

"Circumstances?" The edge of his lip kicked up. "Such

as the effect you had on her?" He sat back and nodded. After a moment, he brushed a hand across his face.

To her surprise, he thanked her for their time, stood up and left.

Evie pushed out a breath. "I believe I need something to drink."

Edgar appeared at the door. "Would you like me to bring some tea, my lady?"

"Oh, heavens. Thank you, Edgar, but I think I need something stronger."

CHAPTER 6

The library

As Tom organized a drink for Evie, she turned to Edgar and asked, "Has Lord Evans left?"

"I'm afraid he has, my lady and..." Edgar's expression changed and now displayed a hint of disapproval. "If I may take the liberty, he did not ask about Lady Evans."

Evie thought there could be a simple explanation. She would not presume to know how Lord Evans' mind worked but it was possible he had made a conscious decision to focus on the case and put his personal matters aside, for the time being, at least.

She knew there were other possible explanations but it really wasn't her place to delve.

Tom handed her a tumbler. Holding it up to her nose, Evie identified the contents as brandy. She cupped the tumbler in her hands, settled back in her chair and tried to empty her mind. The effort didn't get her very far. "Tom, I've been meaning to ask, did you manage to contact Lotte Mannering?"

"Yes, you were right. Lotte Mannering has a contact at the club."

The club.

Evie searched her mind and remembered Edmonds had followed Wilfred Greer to White's.

Tom continued, "It only took her ten minutes to place a telephone call and get back to me. Wilfred Greer was still there. She was going to organize someone to keep an eye on him. With any luck, we'll be able to find out where he is staying in London." Shrugging, he added, "At this point, I'm not really obsessed but merely curious."

As well as relieved, Evie thought. He certainly looked more relaxed than he had earlier on.

"Do you think it's possible he's a regular visitor to town? It's a large city."

"That's what has me intrigued. If, as you suggest, he has visited before, why did I see him today? He's the type of fellow who can make himself invisible in a crowd."

"Heavens, if I wasn't concerned before I think I am now. Do you think he wanted you to see him?"

Tom stretched his legs out and tipped his head back. "I'm most likely reading too much into the encounter."

Evie didn't agree. "It might have been an accidental sighting and he was just as caught off guard as you were."

Nodding, Tom stood up and helped himself to a drink.

Evie closed her eyes and sighed.

She couldn't remember if they'd made plans for that day. So far, the interviews held in the morning had led to meeting someone who was now being held for questioning by the police, followed by the encounter of a familiar yet mysterious man.

Caro's surprise visit should have distracted them. However, she'd been harboring some disturbing news about her marriage.

With the detective's visit fresh in her mind, Evie tried to identify any signs of distress. There had been an air of reserve about him. Restraint, Evie thought. Yes, definitely restraint. He might be focused on the investigation but his thoughts were also engaged on other concerns…

Evie turned her thoughts back to Caro.

She had already made the necessary arrangements for her presentation. If she didn't go through with it, tongues would wag and Henry's worst fears would be realized. Had he thought of that?

She had no doubt in her mind they would eventually sort out their differences and, she hoped, they would come to their senses well before it went too far.

Theirs was a love match. Surely that had to be the strongest foundation of all.

Evie felt a twinge of guilt. In a way, she'd had a hand in Caro's troubles.

If she hadn't become involved in so many cases, then the detective would not have felt compelled to warn his wife…

What had prompted him to do so now?

As she continued to think about Detective Inspector Evans, the mysterious Wilfred Greer sauntered into her thoughts.

With so much information swirling around her mind, Evie found herself drawing parallels between the two men and wondering what their next steps would be if, by some chance, they had both acted without thinking of the consequences.

Everyone knew actions had consequences.

Evie considered the possibility Wilfred Greer had allowed himself to be seen by Tom. Either because he'd wanted to be noticed or because he'd been taken by surprise himself and had lingered in the street corner for longer than intended.

Whatever the reason, now Tom was having him followed. If Wilfred Greer had come to town on some sort of mission, something Evie plucked out of her imagination, Tom would be a step behind him.

"And what of Lord Evans' actions?" Evie whispered. She actually struggled to imagine him acting without knowing precisely what he was doing. His warning to Caro had resulted in Caro taking drastic steps. Had he foreseen such consequences? Evie didn't think so. Maybe that 'something' she couldn't quite put her finger on was the detective's shock at Caro's dramatic exit from his life.

Evie moved on and thought about the process he was employing in the investigation.

He had come to visit her because her name had been mentioned by a suspect.

During their brief chat, he had revealed how little the police knew about Merrin Smith and how unwilling the young woman had been to reveal her employer's name.

Had that been an attempt by Merrin Smith to draw their attention to the investigation without coming straight out and asking for help?

She could ask the same question about Detective Inspector Evans. Despite his obvious reservations about her, he had come to see her.

He had been generous, sharing the little information he had. It could have been a lapse in judgment because his mind was preoccupied with his personal problems or he might have wanted to engage Evie's attention.

"Heavens," she whispered, "I've become a consequence."

She brought the tumbler to her lips only to lower it. "Oh, dear." Her exclamation drew Tom's attention to her. Sitting up, she scattered her previous thoughts and focused on Merrin Smith. "I've just realized something. The detective didn't have any luck getting information about Merrin Smith's employer. I have Merrin Smith's reference. It's bound to have her employer's name."

She looked toward the door but Edgar had left. Instead of ringing for him and asking him to relay a message to Millicent, she set the tumbler down, surged to her feet and went upstairs to her bedroom.

In her room, she went straight to her wardrobe where her handbags sat in a shelf. She rummaged through the handbag she had used that morning but did not find the reference. Hurrying out of her bedroom, she made her way to a small room next to the drawing room which had been designated as Millicent's office.

She found Millicent sitting at a desk, a typewriter in front of her. She had her hands on the keys and, strangely, a piece of paper over her hands.

"Millicent? What on earth are you doing?"

Startled, Millicent sprung back.

Evie apologized for catching her by surprise.

"I'm… oh, this is silly, milady. I'm practicing."

They both looked down at the piece of paper covering the typewriter's keys.

"It's a trick, milady. My fingers are supposed to learn the position of the keys so I can strike them without looking down. You see, I'm not meant to look while I type but I kept cheating. I can't blindfold myself because I need to look at the text I'm typing…"

"So you blindfold your fingers? How cunning."

Millicent grinned. "My index finger is supposed to rest on the letter F as a guide, but sometimes it slips and rests on the letter G which is right next to the F and I end up typing a page full of gobbledygook. As they say, practice makes perfect."

Smiling at Millicent's perseverance and ingenuity, Evie cast her eyes around the office. "Did I return the references to you? I can't remember…"

"Yes, when you changed for luncheon."

"Marvelous. I need Merrin Smith's reference, please."

As Millicent searched for it, Evie wondered how she would use the information.

Of course, she would contact the detective.

However, her curiosity had been piqued.

She would dearly love to know why Merrin Smith had refused to divulge her employer's name. She was being questioned by the police. They must have made the situation clear to her. Murder was a serious matter and the punishment quite severe. She had to realize how much trouble she was in. Why wouldn't she cooperate?

Millicent located the reference and, before handing it to Evie, she asked, "Have you changed your mind about her, milady?"

For a split second, Evie wondered what Millicent would do if she said she had changed her mind and actually wanted to offer the young woman the position. A crisp image emerged in her mind showing Millicent at her most mulish, snatching back the piece of paper, backing away and refusing to hand it over.

The fanciful image dispersed and she suddenly realized something.

"Oh, heavens. You haven't heard the news."

"News?"

"About Merrin Smith." Evie filled her in and told her about the young woman being interviewed by the police.

Millicent's eyes widened. "Never! Really?"

"And that's not all. Lord Evans… Detective Inspector Evans called on us."

Millicent glowered at her typewriter as if casting all blame on it for keeping her in the dark.

Lowering her voice, Evie said, "I'm not sure if I should tell Caro about Lord Evans' visit. Perhaps I'll wait until tomorrow morning. She's bound to be in a better mood then."

Millicent frowned. "Caro? *Lady Evans is here?*" Her cheeks puffed out and her eyes narrowed. "I've been here for hours and no one… meaning, Edgar, bothered to tell me?"

Oh, heavens… Evie floundered and offered a possible explanation for the lapse, "Edgar probably didn't wish to interrupt you."

"Did she even ask to see me? I mean, of course, she's Lady Evans now so she probably doesn't have time for me."

"Nonsense." Evie scooped in a breath. "Caro has a lot on her mind." Her remark did not have the desired effect. Instead of accepting the excuse, Millicent looked puzzled.

It suddenly dawned on Evie that if Millicent hadn't

been aware of Caro's arrival then she wouldn't know anything about Caro's revelation.

Drawing in a fortifying breath, Evie proceeded to give her a brief account, "I'm sorry to be the bearer of ill tidings…"

As she listened, Millicent half rose out of her chair and slumped back down. This happened several times, almost as if she couldn't decide if she should take action or not.

When she finished, Evie admitted, "I honestly don't know what to make of it all."

Sitting back, Millicent surprised her by saying, "We shouldn't meddle. I mean, begging your pardon, milady, I think this is something they should sort out themselves."

Nodding, Evie agreed with her. "I'm relieved to hear you say so, Millicent." Relieved and somewhat surprised because Millicent's sensible advice showed she had certainly come a long way. "I believe she is still processing everything that's happened and that's why she retired to her room but I think she'll be happy to see you. In fact, I know it will do her a world of good. You could try to distract her… take her mind off her problems. But, whatever you do, don't involve her in the case."

"That hardly seems fair," Millicent said. "It would be like taking sides and agreeing with Lord Evans." Her shoulders lowered. "I suppose you're right." She looked at the reference she still held in her hand. "Why would Merrin Smith kill someone?"

"I don't believe the police have actual proof." Evie gave a slow shake of her head. "In any case, we don't know. Apparently, she hasn't revealed anything to the police."

"But she mentioned your name."

"Yes." And that worried Evie.

"Maybe she knows about your reputation," Millicent suggested.

"What do you mean?"

"You're a lady detective. She might think you could get to the truth. Do you think the police would let you speak with her?"

"I don't know. It might be worth a try."

Millicent gave a firm nod. "In her place, I would want you to look into the incident. I'd trust you to find the real culprit." Millicent handed her the reference.

Evie looked at it for a moment and thought there was only one sensible next step. "I should contact Lord Evans... or, rather, Detective Inspector Evans. I must remember to differentiate. Anyhow, this is the information he was after."

"He'll be at the Yard." Reaching for the telephone, Millicent placed the receiver against her ear. When she got through to the operator, she asked for the call to be placed. Handing the telephone to Evie, she sat back and once again glowered at her typewriter.

After a brief wait, the call was picked up. When Evie asked to speak with Detective Inspector Evans, she was told he had already left for the day. That posed a dilemma. She could either wait until the next day or leave a message.

Looking at the piece of paper with the information the detective required, she hesitated.

"Do you have any idea where I can locate him?" Even as she asked the question, she realized she could ask Caro. She would definitely know where her husband stayed while working in London.

The decision was made for her when the policeman refused to give her the information.

Disconnecting the call, she leaned against the desk.

"Millicent, I believe I need a lesson or two in persuasion."

Frowning, Millicent said, "I don't understand why you didn't give him the name."

"No, nor do I." Evie held up the piece of paper. The reference had been handwritten in an elegant script and signed by Lady Barton. "Actually, I think I do know. Call it instinct, if you will. The police did not give a statement and yet Merrin Smith's name appeared in bold print on the front page of the newspaper."

"Are you saying there's an informant in the police?" Millicent asked.

Evie gave a pensive nod. "Yes, I think so. If I'd given the police officer Lady Barton's name, it might have landed in the wrong hands. I don't fancy waking up tomorrow and discovering the name has made the front-page news and been connected to an active murder case. I'm not sure I would want my name bandied about in such a manner. I prefer to pass on the information in person." Straightening, she nodded again. "Yes. I think that will be the best course of action for now. Besides, it's late in the day. The detective is not going to interview Lady Barton tonight." Evie walked to the door. "Millicent, if you're comfortable with the idea, can you please go up and have a chat with Caro?"

Millicent gave a determined nod. "Yes, of course. I'll ask her where he stays in London."

He.

Not Lord Evans or Detective Inspector Evans.

It seemed Millicent had taken sides. Evie wanted to say they shouldn't judge but she couldn't deny Millicent the right to her own opinion.

Standing up, Millicent straightened her dress. "It's not right, milady. He should not have asked that of Caro. It's just not right."

"We don't really know what was behind it all, Millicent. Perhaps he only has Caro's wellbeing in mind. Remember, she has already had one close call. In fact, now that I think about it, he might be right."

Evie returned to the library and found Edgar setting a tray of coffee on the table. Distracted by her thoughts, she said, "Edgar, you should prepare to receive an earful. You were quite remiss in not telling Millicent about Caro's arrival."

Edgar stepped back and lifted his chin. "My lady, Millicent asked not to be disturbed while she practices on her typewriter. She was quite firm about it."

"I see. I won't debate the matter." She saw Tom hiding his smile behind the newspaper. When Edgar left, Evie wagged a finger at Tom. "Look at you, snickering like a school girl."

"I can't help being amused when the servants get the better of you."

"Soon enough, they'll be your servants too."

"And I'll know better than to meddle in their affairs." Sitting up, he set his newspaper down. "Did you find what you were looking for?"

"Oh, yes…" She held up the letter and told him about not being able to pass on the information. Or, rather, being unwilling to do so. "I just didn't feel it was right. Heaven knows I'll probably pay dearly for it."

"So what do you propose doing now?" Tom asked.

"What do you mean?"

"You have the advantage in your hands. If we speak to Lady Barton, we might find out something useful. Once you give Henry that name, it might be difficult to approach her. In fact, given the circumstances, I wouldn't be surprised if he warns you off the case."

Evie drummed her fingers on the armrest. "You want me to stick my nose where it doesn't belong?"

"There must be a reason why Merrin Smith told Henry about you but not about her employer."

"Are you suggesting that might have been her way of drawing my attention and involving me in the case? Millicent made a similar suggestion." She thought about it for a moment. "Surely it's too late in the day to pay Lady Barton a visit." She dropped her gaze and then shifted to the edge of her seat. "Actually, Lady Barton must be wondering where Merrin Smith is. We would be doing her a good turn." She rose to her feet. "That's settled. She lives in Belgravia. That's only a short distance away." She looked down at her pleated skirt. With Millicent busy talking with Caro, she'd be left to her own devices.

What did one wear for such an occasion as barging in on someone to deliver bad news?

CHAPTER 7

On the way to Belgravia

Checking to see she was wearing a matching pair of shoes, Evie made her way downstairs and found Tom waiting for her in the hall. Neither one had dressed for a night on the town. Evie had selected a dark navy-blue dress with a pleated skirt and Tom wore a dark gray suit, white shirt and blue tie. Dressed to blend in, she thought.

As soon as they accomplished their task, they would be returning to Woodridge House for dinner and to hash out the day's events. She imagined it wouldn't take them longer than an hour, if that.

Tom looked up and, as she reached the bottom of the stairs, said, "Edgar has just stepped out for the evening. On his way out, he delivered a message from Millicent. Caro and Henry have a townhouse in Kensington but it's undergoing a few repairs so Henry is staying at the East India Club. Have you heard of it?"

"Yes, of course. It's just off Pall Mall. Nicholas used to stop by sometimes. It's popular with members of Parliament, and military types."

"I thought the East India Company was defunct," Tom said.

"Yes, I believe it has been for quite a number of years. The club has nothing to do with it."

As Tom helped her into her fur lined coat, Evie debated whether or not to call in at the club to speak with Lord Evans. She'd already decided he wouldn't do anything with the information until the next day.

Grimacing, she pictured the encounter. He would no doubt express his disapproval at her unexpected visit, but not in an obvious way. In fact, he might not even reveal how he felt but she would know. Oh, yes. She would definitely know how he felt.

"Countess? Is something wrong?"

Evie harrumphed. "Oh, I suppose we must do the right thing and pay Lord Evans a visit."

"Is that why you grimaced?"

She tried to adopt a neutral expression. "If you must know, I have reservations about gentlemen's clubs. I simply do not understand the need for men to be so exclusive. I imagine they get up to all sorts of mischief."

"I wouldn't know." Tom grinned. "Remember, I'm relatively new to all this."

Yes, but Evie knew he was in a position to enter that world. Would he?

"I doubt it," he said, almost as if he'd read her mind.

"You always seem to know what I'm thinking. How do you do that? I can't possibly be so transparent."

"You responded with a slight, querying lift of your eyebrow which also held a hint of derision."

"I had no idea my eyebrows were so expressive."

Tom chortled. "Anyhow, you needn't fear about me joining one of those male bastions of exclusivity. I doubt they welcome what you might call the *nouveau riche*."

"Tom, I would never use that term to refer to you. There's nothing ostentatious about you."

They walked out of the North Audley Street house and into the early evening chill. While the days had been mostly clear and sunny, spring was a couple of weeks away.

Looking up, Evie expected to find Edmonds standing by the Duesenberg, ready to drive them to Belgravia. Instead, she saw a roadster.

Tom held the passenger door open for her. Evie then waited for Tom to round the car and settle in to ask, "Is this your new town motor-car?"

Tom brushed his hand along the steering wheel. "It's a Duesenberg Straight Eight."

"You already have a roadster."

"Now I have two." He lifted an eyebrow. "Are you trying to make a point?"

"You risk making Edmonds redundant. His feelings will be hurt."

"Henrietta and the others keep him busy." He tilted his head and narrowed his eyes. "Is that a new hat?"

"It hardly bears comparison…" Grinning, she adjusted her new hat. "Do you like it?"

"Midnight blue. It matches the new car." He leaned in and murmured, "Feeling better?"

"Yes, it always helps to chatter about nothing. If I didn't, I'd succumb to the whirlpool of thoughts taking up residence in my mind."

As Tom pulled away, she glanced up at the second-floor window and wondered how Millicent was faring. Caro could be stubborn and so could Millicent. However, even in the midst of a disagreement they could bond over the silliest thing.

"Do you remember how Caro broke the news of her engagement to us?" Tom asked.

Evie's lips curved up. "How could I forget?" Caro had wailed as she'd announced the news.

Tom leaned in and asked, "Have you ever seen such a dramatic performance?"

"A performance? I've never thought of it in those terms but I suppose you're right. It was quite melodramatic. Her emotions must have been at breaking point. Not only had she received a proposal of marriage but the offer came with a title and a swift elevation for Caro." From lady's maid to Lady Evans, Evie thought. "It was all perfectly understandable. Oh… are you trying to make a point?" Had he noticed her looking up at Caro's bedroom window?

Tom settled back in his seat. "I suppose I am. As level-headed as she is, Caro can also be swept away by her emotions. I have no doubt this is nothing but a silly quarrel."

When he made a turn, she asked, "Do you know where you're going?"

"Edmonds explained the quickest route. Do you have a

plan?"

She was only thinking about letting Lady Barton know her maid had been taken into police custody. "I suppose we'll play it by ear. The house lights might give us a hint as to how we might proceed. Lady Barton might be dining at home or entertaining."

It was early evening—that strange, in-between time when the residential streets fell silent as people prepared for dinner or an evening out. "Lady Barton might be spending the evening out on the town. I'm hoping that's the case, that way we can be assured of finding her at home readying herself to go out."

Tom snorted. "And we'll arrive just in time to ruin her evening."

"We don't exactly have a choice, Tom. In any case, this might give us an opportunity to ask a few questions. That's not to say I've come up with any."

All too soon, they arrived at the Belgravia address. Tom brought the motor to a stop outside a row of elegantly proportioned white stucco terraced townhouses and searched for the right number.

He pointed to a house with dim lights illuminating the windows. "Now what?"

Evie considered their options. She could ask Tom to test the waters. For all they knew, they might be refused entry. Tapping her handbag, she considered using out one of two calling cards. She had one for Lady Woodridge and another one with her maiden name, Evie Parker. Millicent had been instrumental in digging it out of the back of a wardrobe and suggesting she could use the card for her lady detective enterprise.

"She needs to be informed so we should be prepared to be as persuasive as possible."

Tom shifted and looked at her. "What exactly does that mean? Are you suggesting I should be ready and willing to thrust my foot against the door as it's slammed in our faces?"

Nibbling the edge of her lip to stop herself from laughing, she gave him a small nod. "If it comes to that. Your shoes are sturdier than mine."

As Tom emerged from the motor and walked around to open the passenger door, Evie entertained a few doubts. In the end, she convinced herself Lady Barton needed to know tonight. If they had taken the time to look for Detective Inspector Evans at his club, there would have been no guarantee of finding him there. How much time would they have wasted?

"I take full responsibility," Evie said as she stepped out of the motor car.

Trying to make sense of her remark, Tom asked, "Have you been arguing with yourself?"

"Yes, of course. I rather enjoy it because I always win, no matter which side I take."

"I assume you take both sides."

"Precisely."

They walked up to the front steps and stopped for a moment. They were about to barge in on a complete stranger and tell them their maid was in police custody.

How would Lady Barton react?

Most people she knew dreaded the possibility of a scandal. Also, when bad news was delivered, people usually went straight into denial. That would then require a great deal of explaining.

"I dutifully hand over the reins to you, Lady Woodridge."

Evie nodded. "Right… well, it's now or never."

They walked up the steps and Tom rang the bell.

Evie had come across dozens of butlers but none as aloof as the one who opened Lady Barton's door.

His mouth was downturned and his long nose held high as he tilted his head up, literally looking down his nose at them.

Evie introduced herself as Lady Woodridge and asked to speak with Lady Barton.

The butler gave them both a measured look which spoke of ambivalence and a desire to slam the door in their faces.

"Lady Woodridge, the Countess of Woodridge, to be precise," Tom said in what sounded like a warning snarl.

Despite his unfriendly demeanor, the butler showed them through to the drawing room, saying he would see if her ladyship was at home.

"At home? What exactly does that mean?" Tom complained as they sat down to wait for Lady Barton. "Either he knows she's home or he doesn't."

At the same time, Evie murmured, "Really, Tom? The Countess of Woodridge?"

Tom swiftly defended himself. "What good is having a title if you're not going to use it?"

"I'll remember that when you receive your knighthood."

His eyes glinted. "I thought Henrietta was aiming higher. Actually, I have been meaning to ask. What exactly did she mean by that?"

"She was probably thinking of a baronetcy."

"Isn't that an inherited title?"

"No, it can be given for services to the crown. Just like the knighthood."

"Oh, I see. That makes sense. I remember Henrietta saying something about me saving a royal's life. I think she might have been trying to decide on the best person to injure the royal so that I could then save them. Of course, I don't for a moment believe she would go to such lengths." He glanced at Evie. "Some sort of reassurance would be greatly appreciated. I don't fancy ending up in prison."

They heard the sound of approaching footsteps. They were hurried at first and then they slowed down as they drew closer and finally came to a stop just outside the door. Evie imagined Lady Barton taking a moment to collect her thoughts.

Tom leaned in and whispered, "She might be wondering where she's heard the name and, right about now, it's come to her. You're that troublemaking countess. The notorious Lady Woodridge."

The drawing room door opened and the butler stepped in. A few seconds later, a woman entered. Dressed in a dark burgundy evening gown and a matching headband, she had clearly been preparing to go out for the evening.

"Lady Woodridge." The woman looked understandably puzzled by their presence.

"Lady Barton," Evie smiled, introduced Tom and apologized for the intrusion.

Lady Barton looked from one to the other. "May I ask what this is about?"

"Yes, of course," Evie said. "However, I need to confirm something first."

Lady Barton nodded.

"Is Merrin Smith in your employ?"

Lady Barton's eyebrows drew down. "Y-yes, she is. Do you wish to speak with her?"

The butler cleared his throat. When Lady Barton ignored him, he cleared his throat again. "Begging your pardon, my lady. Smith hasn't returned yet."

Smith? Evie was about to correct the butler when she remembered lady's maids were usually referred to by their family names rather than their first names.

"She hasn't?"

Evie found Lady Barton's reaction utterly perplexing. She assumed Merrin was employed as her lady's maid. Merrin's job would be to assist Lady Barton in dressing. How could she not know she hadn't returned? Then she remembered Millicent saying Merrin Smith had been seen going out every evening, but that could have happened after attending to her duties…

Lady Barton looked at Evie and spread her hands out in a gesture of ignorance.

"Actually, Lady Barton, I know Merrin Smith is not here."

The woman's eyebrows hitched up in surprise.

Evie studied her as she said, "She is currently being held for questioning by the police."

Lady Barton's cheeks paled. She shot the butler a quick glance. "Preston, would you leave us, please?"

The butler nodded and exited the drawing room.

When they were left alone, Lady Barton reached for a

chair and sat down on the edge, opposite Tom and Evie. "How do you come to know that?"

For the second time that day, Evie provided a brief summary of events. "The police haven't been able to get any information out of her. They specifically wanted to know her employer's name."

Lady Barton looked at Evie without blinking. "You haven't said what she stands accused of doing."

"No formal charges have been issued. The police think she is involved in Mrs. Colliers' death. Are you familiar with her?"

Lady Barton pressed her hand to her chest. Taking a deep swallow, she gave a brisk shake of her head. "Do you happen to know how Mrs. Colliers died?"

Evie glanced at Tom. "Actually, no, we don't." She engraved the question in her mind and hoped to remember to ask Lord Evans.

"Lady Barton... Merrin Smith appears to be looking for another position. Did you know about that?"

She gave a distracted nod. "We have plans to go abroad and Smith doesn't care to travel."

Evie considered the possibility Mrs. Colliers had been interviewing for a maid. That might justify Merrin being seen close to her home. She then remembered Tom saying Merrin had left the pub like a bat out of hell. Had she been in a hurry to reach her next appointment?

Frowning, Lady Barton asked, "How exactly did you come into possession of my name?"

"You wrote a reference for Merrin Smith and I interviewed her this morning. That's how I came to learn of her fate. I saw the newspaper—"

Lady Barton shot to her feet. "Newspaper?"

Evie nodded. "There's a brief article on the front page of the afternoon edition."

Lady Barton rang the bell. Several seconds later, the butler appeared at the door. "Preston, do we have the afternoon edition?"

"I'm afraid there was a slight accident in the kitchen involving some spillage and the newspaper is ruined, my lady. I didn't think anything of it because Lord Barton is the only one who reads it and…"

"Yes, yes. I see." Lady Barton wrung her hands together.

"Would you like me to procure another copy, my lady?"

"No, that won't be necessary, Preston. Thank you, that will be all."

The butler dipped his head and exited the room.

Lady Barton stood watching the door and, in Evie's opinion, she employed the moment to collect herself. Her posture remained perfectly erect and still. The fact it took her a moment to turn suggested she hadn't been ready to face Evie again.

Why would that be?

Did she have something to hide? Or was she merely in shock and trying to come to grips with the unexpected situation?

Evie could tell the moment Lady Barton decided to turn. She drew in a deep breath and her shoulders rose slightly and then lowered.

When she finally turned, her expression was blank. At least, Evie thought, she wasn't smiling and pretending nothing had happened.

"Lady Barton, I hope you don't feel I'm intruding but I

must ask. How did you not know your maid had not returned?" Evie had no idea if Lady Barton knew of her involvement in several crimes. Evie hoped she didn't. She also hoped Lady Barton would see the question as mere curiosity.

Lady Barton made a dismissive gesture with her hand. "Since Smith doesn't wish to travel with me, I have been relying on another maid so she becomes familiar with the way I like things done." She walked to the chair and sat down again, wrapping her hands around the armrests. "Oh, my goodness. Smith will be spending the night in prison."

Evie felt a rush of heat rise up to her cheeks. She had no idea where Merrin was and absolutely no concept of what she was experiencing at the moment. And, worse, she hadn't given it a moment's thought, until now.

Overcome with a sense of guilt and urgency, Evie handed Lady Barton her card. "Detective Inspector Evans will no doubt call on you tomorrow. I suspect he will have more questions for you." She glanced at the card she had just handed her. "If you think of anything that might be important, I can be reached at that number. If I'm not available, my secretary, Millicent, can be trusted to take a message."

As they made their way out, Evie thought about the one question which now took center stage in her mind.

Why had Lady Barton lied about not knowing Mrs. Colliers?

CHAPTER 8

The East India Club
St James's London

*E*vie did not share her suspicion about Lady Barton lying. Mostly because it was based on pure instinct. Also, as they made their way to the gentlemen's club in St James's, her thoughts were fixated on Merrin Smith.

She imagined her facing all sorts of horrors and being traumatized by the unfamiliar experience of being in prison and not knowing what her fate would be.

Suddenly, she could think of nothing else but finding a way to improve the young woman's situation, and the only way to do that would be to bring the matter to the detective's attention and, most importantly, use the information she had as a bartering tool. As one should, she thought.

Yes, she would reveal the identity of Merrin's employer to Detective Inspector Evans but only on the condition that he take immediate action to ensure the young woman spent her time in custody in relative comfort.

Innocent until proven guilty, she thought.

Having made that decision, she moved on to other thoughts.

"Tom?"

Keeping his eyes on the road, he leaned toward her.

"How far do you think Lyall Street is from Lady Barton's home?"

"Lyall Street?"

"Lyall Street, Belgravia," she clarified. "I'm sure that's where the detective said Mrs. Collier lived."

Hearing him say it was only a few minutes' walk from Belgrave Square sent a shiver up Evie's spine.

Lady Barton lived around the corner from Belgrave Square.

Tom found a space for the motor car and they both sat back and looked at the building. All the lights were on at the club and they could distinguish the shape of people moving about inside.

"Did we just drive along Green Park?" she asked.

Tom nodded. "Are you wondering at the proximity of all these addresses?"

"Yes. Belgravia and the club are only separated by a few streets and the park."

He signaled up ahead. "And Woodridge House is up that way, within easy walking distance." He smiled. "It's all rather cozy." He straightened his tie. "I suppose I should go in and hunt down Henry."

"Tom, this is business. He's not Henry or even Lord Evans. He's Detective Inspector Evans."

Tom laughed. "I'm sure you have a few alternative names for him floating around your head, but you're a well brought up lady who won't succumb to gutter language."

Evie lifted her chin. "You forget, Mr. Winchester, I was a hoyden. I'm sure I'm quite capable…" She huffed out a breath. When she spoke, her voice hitched, "*How dare he warn Caro against me?*"

Tom laughed. "I knew it was bound to come out sooner or later. Are you feeling better?"

Evie shifted in her seat and gave her coat sleeve a firm tug. "I keep telling myself Henry acted out of love for Caro and concern for her wellbeing. Heaven knows, I've had more than my fair share of critics and I always dismiss them as insignificant bores, but this is too close to home. Also, it's not really about me. I'm more concerned about Caro because she clearly wishes to involve herself in investigations and he is stifling her efforts. You could almost say he is shackling her. Actually, it would be more precise to say he is hobbling her."

Her last remarks caught her by surprise. She'd had no idea she'd been harboring those opinions. Evie hoped it didn't mean Caro had found a void in her life because that could lead to a lifetime of regrets and unhappiness.

She drew in a deep breath. "Yes, I'm feeling better now."

"Shall we proceed?" he asked.

Evie nodded and waved her hand toward the club. "As Henrietta would say, *tally-ho!*"

Tom emerged from the motor car and buttoned his

coat. "Wish me luck."

"Wait!"

Frowning, he rounded the motor car and leaned down. "Last minute instructions?"

"Yes." Evie glanced at the club and the porter standing on the front porch. He looked rather formidable in this dark coat and top hat. "I'm coming with you."

Tom shot upright and looked at the club entrance. "Is that a good idea, Countess?"

"Good or bad, I am coming along, Tom. This business of keeping women out is utter nonsense." Instead of waiting for Tom to decide if he would open the passenger door or not, she went ahead and did it herself.

"Don't you think it might be best if I go in first and locate Henry? We could arrange to meet nearby. I think there's a quaint little restaurant not far from here. Or perhaps a pub…"

"You would have me skulking about in the darkness? Hiding in the shadows?" Evie snorted and gave her glove a firm tug. "Tom, I have decided to make a statement… To take a stand… This is my chance to kill two birds with one stone."

"All right. You sound determined."

"Oh, I am, quite determined. In fact, I might even go so far as to say I am obsessively and *irrevocably* determined."

Tom hummed. "Irrevocably."

"I would ask you to move closer to the lamppost but I don't need to because I can hear the laughter in your tone."

Tom cleared his throat. "I believe what you heard was actually nervous laughter. But, not to worry, I am up for the challenge."

"Glad to hear that." Evie smiled at him. "I need to deliver vital information to the detective in charge of an investigation. This is the most expedient way of doing it. Certainly not by engaging a proxy."

Tom slipped his hands inside his pocket. "Well, if you think about it, there are other ways which might be even more expedient. I'm thinking of perhaps avoiding the scene which will inevitable ensue the moment you set foot inside that club, the scene which will actually delay the delivery of the information. The very scene which will draw anyone within hearing into an argument."

Evie harrumphed.

"Oh, yes," Tom continued. "I can picture it quite clearly." He cleared his throat, lifted his chin and provided an excellent imitation of several club members stepping forward to state their objections. "Now, see here, Stevens. We pay you good money to keep riffraff and women out of our club. Do your job." Lowering his voice, he added in a nasal tone, "Are the sacred halls of our brotherhood to be thus polluted." Leaning in, he lowered his voice. "Good heavens, it's that countess everyone's been talking about... the notorious Lady Woodridge. What the devil is she doing here. Has someone been murdered in their bed?"

Evie knew he made a valid point. Her presence was bound to cause a stir and draw unnecessary attention to herself. That would, in turn, cause a delay in delivering the information to Lord Evans. Worse still, it could result in her name being plastered in the front page of the morning newspaper.

And yet...

"I am determined."

"Very well." Tom cupped her elbow only to withdraw

his hand. "Perhaps you don't wish me to assist you across the street."

Hiding her smile, Evie darted him a look. "Do I look like an invalid?"

"No, indeed, you do not. However, good manners compel me to extend the courtesy."

"You are still poking fun at me. Good for you. If we are to get through this, we'll need a good dose of good humor. Onward, Mr. Winchester."

Tom cupped her elbow and surged ahead, saying, "The Countess of Woodridge storms Gentlemen's Club. Oh, yes. That will be a sparkling headline."

They hurried along to clear the way for a motor car approaching at top speed. Reaching the steps, they continued on without stopping.

"Are you breathing?" Tom whispered.

"Just barely." Her heart punched against her chest. She knew they ran the very real risk of being stopped and, perhaps, even prevented from entering the club.

With her eyes lowered to ensure she didn't trip, she just managed to catch a glimpse of the doorman. He shifted his feet and stared straight at Tom.

"Bradford?" she heard Tom ask and then say, "I called ahead. This is an urgent matter." His tone was commanding, brisk and to the point.

"No, not Bradford, sir... You probably mean Rogers and he's not here at the moment."

Still sounding supremely confident, Tom exclaimed, "Oh, I was told Bradford. I'm sure of it. Then again, there was a lot of noise around me and the line crackled. As I said, it's an urgent matter."

To Evie's surprise, the doorman drew the door open for them.

As Tom swept her through, he reached inside his pocket, drew something out and handed it to the doorman. Evie assumed he'd just handed over a substantial amount of money.

"Well done, Tom."

"Yes, thank you. Now what?"

They stepped right into the spacious hall with wood paneled walls and paintings of very serious looking gentlemen. There were three sets of double doors, one at the end of the hall and the other two at the sides.

"Door number one, two or three?" Tom asked.

"I daresay it will be decided for us," Evie suggested. "Someone is bound to rush out and tackle us to the ground."

As expected, a man dressed in black tails and a waistcoat with horizontal stripes in gold and burgundy emerged from the back room and headed directly toward them, his pace quite brisk. He wore white gloves so Evie assumed he was the club's butler.

Coming to a stop, he tucked both hands behind his back and lifted his chin. "May I help you?" he asked Tom and barely spared Evie a glance.

"It's an urgent matter. We are here to see Lord Evans. Or, rather, Detective Inspector Evans. He will be glad you announced us."

"Will he, indeed?"

Tom's jaws clenched. "Yes, he will be, indeed.

The butler's eyebrows almost hit the roof.

Tom's mouth firmed.

Evie had recently discovered he carried a holstered

revolver and, at that moment, she wondered if he had just given the man a glimpse of it.

"Your name, sir."

"Tom Winchester."

"Very well. If you would please wait here." He swung on his heels and went through one of the side doors. The moment he opened it, Evie picked up the sweet scent of cigars. Several heads turned to see who was entering and, in that split second, Evie saw two men she recognized. Both titled and both quite short-sighted. As she looked at them, they squinted as if trying to clear their eyes.

Before Evie could capture their reactions, the door closed.

"Mr. Winchester, you were superb," she murmured.

Tom looked at her, his expression quite stern.

Heavens.

Winking at her, he smiled. "Don't distract me, I need to stay in character. We might not be out of the woods just yet."

The doors directly in front of them opened and a man with white hair and moustache walked out, his formal attire identifying him as a club member.

Walking across the hall and heading toward the side doors, he looked at Evie and then at Tom. Suddenly, his expression changed and he raised a finger as if to suggest he had made the connection. Distracted, he nearly collided with a pedestal. Sidestepping it, he hurried along.

"I bet you a shilling he recognized me and is about to spread the news," Evie said.

"A shilling? That's hardly worth the trouble."

"Well, I'm sorry, but that's all I carry in my bag. I saw

the coin today as I rummaged through my bag. I have no idea how it got there…"

"He certainly recognized you. Where do you think he's seen you?"

Evie thought about all the guests who had traipsed through Halton House or the hunting lodge over the years. Too many faces, too many people to name.

The door opened again and Lord Evans emerged. He stopped for a moment and looked at them as if he couldn't quite believe his eyes.

Evie was about to give him a challenging look when she diverted her attention and glanced just past his shoulder.

Evie focused her gaze on someone she recognized sitting on a leather chair by the fireplace.

She nudged Tom.

"Yes, I see him."

Tom still had her elbow cupped in his hand so he drew her a couple of steps back, enough to move them out of sight of the man they had both just recognized.

Lord Evans gave a stiff nod and approached them. Noticing their attention on the door and the room beyond, he turned slightly but the door behind him closed.

Lifting her chin, Evie greeted him. "Detective Inspector Evans, thank you for agreeing to see us."

The door opened again and someone peered out. Cigar smoke wafted out and Evie imagined everyone taking an anxious puff and blowing smoke out as they expressed their objections to the sacrilegious assault on their stronghold. As if to confirm it, Evie heard a rise in voices carrying a hint of protestation.

The detective tucked his hands behind his back. "I was told there were two angry people demanding to see me on an urgent matter and wouldn't take no for an answer."

Evie and Tom exchanged a glance.

Frowning, Tom said, "I'm sure I wasn't that forceful."

"No, not at all and you didn't sound angry," Evie concurred.

The detective glanced at Evie and raised an eyebrow.

"Don't look at me. I did not even speak."

Releasing a long breath, the detective looked around and then signaled to a door Evie hadn't noticed. As he led them toward it, Evie nudged Tom and mouthed, "We're in."

The detective showed them through to a wood paneled office lined with bookshelves filled with leather bound books and a desk with a couple of chairs. He invited them to sit while he leaned against the desk and crossed his arms.

"I take it you have some important news related to the case," he said.

Evie nodded but instead of giving him the information, she thought about what she wanted from him. She had choices. She knew how to ask for something. Her status actually provided her with many advantages. In this instance, she knew she'd have to tread with care because she was dealing with a police officer who held certain opinions about her.

"We most certainly do have some news for you. Or, rather, information. However," her voice rose and firmed. "First I need you to promise me Merrin Smith will be well looked after whilst in police custody."

Surprised by her demand, Tom shot her a disbelieving glance, while the detective merely frowned.

Surging onwards, Evie added, "In fact, I would like her to be given what you might call special privileges. I imagine prison food is not exactly palatable and I also imagine the cells are cold."

The detective now scowled at Evie.

He crossed his arms and leaned forward. "Correct me if I'm wrong, Lady Woodridge, it sounds to me as if you are trying to coerce me into doing your bidding in exchange for the information you hold."

Evie's tone softened and she smiled. "That might be one way of looking at it."

"And if I don't meet your demands?"

Evie lifted her chin even higher, held his gaze for a moment and then declared, "I might experience a memory lapse."

The detective's voice lowered and filled with disbelief. "You are bartering with an officer of the law?"

Evie shrugged. "I am negotiating."

He held her gaze until Evie felt the need to shift in her seat. Not that she did. In fact, she refused to show any sign of discomfort.

They both fell silent. Neither one blinked.

Suddenly, the detective stood upright. "Very well. I'll see to it that she receives a hearty meal and a thick blanket."

Evie gave a stiff nod. "You should do it now. The poor girl must be famished and shivering with cold, not to mention feeling terrified."

The detective pinched the bridge of his nose.

Evie imagined Tom chortling and saying she'd given Lord Evans a migraine.

Without saying a word, he swung around, went to sit at the desk and placed a telephone call. He delivered the order in a crisp tone and was about to end the call when the person at the other end must have asked a question. "Peabody, I don't know, just do it." He set the telephone aside and sat back, his hands clasped in front of him.

Evie found herself wondering if she could actually trust him to have made the telephone call. What if he'd only just pretended to do it in order to humor her?

She managed to talk herself out of the suspicion but only because his frustration looked too real and on the verge of exploding.

Opening her handbag, she drew out the reference with Merrin Smith's employer's name and address written on it.

She was about to hand it to him when Tom reached for her hand.

"Wait," Tom said.

The detective's eyes widened. "I take it you have demands of your own."

"As a matter of fact, yes, I do."

"And you are going to use the information as a bartering tool? Do you realize I could place you both under arrest for withholding evidence?"

Instead of being cowed into compliance, Tom continued, "There is a man in the clubroom. He's sitting by the fireplace and wearing a navy blue and red tie. His name is Wilfred Greer."

The detective's mouth firmed. His lips barely moved when he said, "What about him?"

"Tom thinks he's a suspicious character and is up to no good," Evie declared.

The detective fell silent and looked down at his hands.

He hadn't asked for a clear description of Wilfred Greer. That suggested he actually knew him.

This time, Evie swore he spoke through gritted teeth.

"You don't need to worry about him."

When Tom didn't say anything, Evie spoke up, "Does that mean you know him and can assure us he is in London for pleasure and not business?" Before he could answer, she added, "Is he staying here?" That meant he was a member.

Tom released her hand. Evie took that to mean he wanted her to hand over the reference. "Are you sure?"

Tom nodded.

Evie looked down at the reference. She still held the upper hand, so to speak. Such opportunities did not come by every day. Should she extract an apology from Lord Evans for suggesting she was a bad influence and, while she was at it, should she try to gain some sort of concession for Caro?

Grumbling under her breath, she remembered she and Millicent had agreed they shouldn't meddle in the couple's quarrel.

"Oh, very well." Evie handed him the piece of paper. "You should know, we have already spoken with Lady Barton. She didn't even know Merrin Smith hadn't returned from her outing. Indeed, she had no idea her lady's maid had been taken into custody. I'm sure she'll have something to say about that."

He took the letter and frowned. "Did you say Lady Barton?"

CHAPTER 9

*D*etective Inspector Evans had recognized Lady Barton's name.

The suggestion had been in the way he'd phrased his question and in his intonation. In any other conversation, he might have said, '*Oh, I know Lady Barton. Or... Lady Barton. That's interesting. Her name has recently cropped up as a person of interest.*'"

"He knows Lady Barton," Evie murmured as they made their way out of the club.

When she'd asked the detective if he was familiar with the name, he had folded the reference letter and had tucked it inside his coat pocket. Gesturing to the door, the detective had then escorted them right up to the front door, almost as if he had taken it upon himself to ensure they left the premises.

"I only noticed he didn't thank you for the information," Tom said. "Something is definitely wrong with him."

Evie agreed and she feared it had something to do

with the detective's perception of her changing quite dramatically.

As they reached the roadster, she recalled the conversation they had walked in on earlier that day. Henrietta had claimed they each had a different way of perceiving her because opinions varied.

Evie suspected the detective had changed whatever opinion he'd held about her, and the new opinion was less than complimentary.

Of course, being a gentleman meant that he would remain civil and that would be quite telling as his manner toward her would reveal extreme reserve rather than unreserved friendliness.

Every time he greeted her and asked how she was, she would know his mind would be entertaining thoughts of her escapades.

"What now?" Tom asked.

"We need to put everything into perspective and we should take advantage of the peace and quiet while we can. Henrietta and the others have gone out for the evening but they could return at any moment."

They drove the short distance in silence, their brows furrowed as they tossed around the information they'd collected.

Evie hoped one or the other would come up with something significant, if not that evening then the next morning. In her experience, and with so much always going on around her, sometimes it took a good night's rest before thoughts could surface with any clarity.

When Tom brought the motor car to a stop outside Woodridge House, Evie asked him to wait a moment before going inside.

"I just want to see if anyone comes to the window."

"In other words," Tom said, "We're the scouting party."

"It pays to be forewarned."

The lights in the front rooms were dim, suggesting only a few table lamps were turned on and she could see a couple of soft lights in the upstairs rooms. She supposed Caro and Millicent were still chatting.

Since the front door remained closed, she assumed no one had noticed them.

Tom murmured, "Edgar went to the theater."

"Oh, yes, of course." Whenever they were in town, he made a point of attending as many performances as he could, with or without Millicent, who didn't quite share his enthusiasm for the theater.

"Where do you think the detective heard Lady Barton's name?" she asked.

Tom shrugged. "Earlier today, we both got the impression he didn't know much about the case because he couldn't even get Merrin Smith to provide the most basic information. Now..." Tom shook his head. "I'm not so sure."

"Are you suggesting he might actually know more than he's letting on?" Evie gasped. "Oh, of course. When he first arrived, I thought he looked disheveled but not in an untidy way. I just couldn't put my finger on it. Now, I'm thinking..." Evie hummed.

"What?"

"He must have so much information swimming around his head and then there's the quarrel with Millicent. I think it's all having an effect on his general demeanor. He's radiating a feeling of being disheveled." Although, at the club he had looked relaxed. In his milieu, she supposed and hoped it would do him a world of good. If he could refresh his mind, he might come to realize how wrong he'd been telling Caro she couldn't take an interest in investigations.

Tom gave a nod of understanding. "When you're struck by the same condition, your eyes widen slightly, your lips part as if you're about to gasp and you tend to look surprised."

"Really?"

He looked at her and squinted. "I think you're doing it now."

Shrugging, Evie said, "I wouldn't necessarily call it a condition."

Tom chortled. "Fine, it's a state of perplexity."

"Anyhow, yes, I think he might know more but with everything going on, he just doesn't have any room in his head to decide what he can or can't tell us so he's not revealing anything at all." Evie collected her handbag. "I think the coast is clear."

Reaching the front steps, Tom said, "What exactly are we going to do about dinner?"

She hadn't given it any thought, but now that they'd arrived, she realized the servants who had not gone out for the evening would be enjoying their dinner.

"I'll be happy with a piece of cheese and some bread," Evie suggested.

Tom opened the front door and stepped aside to let her through. "I think I've just had a bright business idea."

"You sound excited. What is it?"

"Milk and other products are delivered to the door. Why not deliver meals as well?"

"That sounds rather good, but what would happen to the people working in the kitchen here?"

"They could have a day free to do what they wanted. Or, they could sit down to a leisurely dinner without you imposing demands on them to fetch you a hunk of bread and cheese."

"Oh, I was actually thinking of sneaking into the kitchen and fetching it myself. I do know my way to the kitchen."

He helped her out of her coat and they made their way to the library.

Setting their coats aside on a chair, he joined Evie by the fireplace. While Evie made herself comfortable, he remained standing, his thoughts still on his bright idea.

"What's wrong?" she asked.

Instead of answering, he walked with purpose to the desk in the corner and picked up the telephone.

While curious, she managed to tune out and focus on the detective's behavior. Although, when she heard Tom asking to be connected to The Criterion, she sat up and shifted to look at him.

He had a brief conversation during which he mentioned a generous amount of money for placing such a request. Ending the call, he joined her and sat opposite her, his eyes brimming with joy.

"I take it our humble piece of cheese and bread has been upgraded to a sumptuous meal," Evie remarked.

He nodded and smiled with satisfaction.

"I won't ask how you managed it because I heard you offer a large amount of money."

He looked at his watch. "Dinner should be served in about forty-five minutes."

Evie stood up and walked across to the desk where she found some paper and a fountain pen.

Taking her place by the fireplace, she smoothed out the piece of paper. "Let's earn it, shall we?"

Tom brushed his hand across his chin. "I think you might be right. Henry knows more than he's letting on and he definitely sounded surprised to learn the name of Merrin's employer."

"Yes, but what does that mean?" Evie made a note of it. "What about his reaction to Wilfred Greer?"

"Yes, I found that odd. I'm sure we can safely assume he knows him and, more significantly, he knows *of* him."

"Meaning, Wilfred Greer's reputation precedes him?"

Tom gave a pensive nod.

"But how do we interpret all that? Do we assume the detective feels confident about Wilfred Greer and knows he's not here to cause trouble or…" She drummed her fingers on the armrest.

"Or?" he prompted.

"Or, do we let our imagination run wild and think the detective knows why Wilfred Greer is in London? That's assuming he knows a great deal about him, and I'm willing to bet he does."

Tom steepled his fingers under his chin. "There was something about the way Henry looked down at his hands before answering. Almost as if he spent some time considering what he would say."

Evie snorted and complained, "He didn't say anything."

Tom smiled. "How dare he keep us in the dark."

"Indeed. It's bad enough he has conflicting opinions about me…"

"I see, now they're conflicting. How did that happen?"

Evie shifted in her seat. "I'm sure, at some point, he found me delightful and quite competent. He's only now formed a new opinion of me, I'm sure of it, and it is causing all sorts of confusion in his mind."

Tom tipped his head back and laughed. "The poor man. He must be feeling wretched holding so many thoughts about you."

"It would serve him right." Evie set her paper and pen aside and walked over to the desk. Finding what she wanted, she returned and settled down to look through her copy of *Debrett's*.

"Who are you looking up?"

"Barton. Here it is. Lord Barton is a baron. He is Elliot Quincy, the 5th Baron Barton. The title was created in 1812 for one of his ancestors, a civil servant by the name of Sir John Quincy."

"And Lady Barton's husband is Elliot Quincy," Tom murmured.

"Yes, Elliot Quincy, Lord Barton. Does the name ring a bell? Has it ever cropped up in the newspapers?"

"I'm not sure. Lady Barton has been mentioned several times today. It's difficult to tell."

"Speaking of Lady Barton," Evie set the book aside. "Did you notice the way Lady Barton cut her butler off in mid-sentence? He was just about to say something about Lord Barton."

"Yes, at the time, I assumed it had something to do with the newspaper and Lord Barton being the only one who read it. At least, that's what I imagine the butler had been about to say."

Evie held up a finger. "And when something spilled on

the newspaper, the butler didn't bother replacing it because…"

Tom picked up the thread, "Because Lord Barton was not there to read it?"

As they stared at each other Evie thought how much she loved their tandem conversations.

"I don't know what it means but I would dearly love to know where Lord Barton is. Away on business? In the country? Fishing? Shooting? Those are the usual activities that lure titled gentlemen away from their townhouses." Evie wrote his name down and put a question mark next to it. Looking up, she couldn't help adding, "Then again, his absence might have a greater significance."

"What if Lady Barton interrupted the butler simply because the information was superfluous and she just wanted to get on with the conversation she was having with you?"

"That would make sense," Evie agreed. "But you know we mustn't discount anything. I'm going to list every person we come across or hear about. It's too early to dismiss anyone."

She skimmed through what she'd written only to look up and straight at the library door. Tom did likewise, swiveling in his seat.

They heard the front door opening and someone walking in, followed by several other footsteps.

Evie and Tom stilled.

He lowered his voice to a murmur, "I didn't order enough food to share."

"That's your first thought?" Evie rolled her eyes.

He shifted forward and whispered, "Think about it. They're back early. Either they canceled their dinner plans or their outing to the theater or the opera or wherever they were going tonight. If they canceled dinner, they'll be hungry and I'm willing to bet anything they will not settle for a piece of cheese and a hunk of bread."

"Tom, do we not feed you enough?"

He sat back and crossed his arms. "I can't remember luncheon. My mind was occupied with other matters." His shoulders lowered. "My apologies, Countess. There are times when hunger precedes good manners."

"This is so unlike you."

Tom frowned and sounded worried when he said, "I know. I don't even recognize myself."

"Do you think seeing Wilfred Greer triggered something?"

His eyes widened. "I can't imagine what that might be."

Perhaps he had triggered a bad memory of going hungry, Evie thought. "You know him from the trenches." For most people, it had been the worst experience of their lives…

Hearing the sound of footfalls softening, Evie pressed a finger to her lips. She signaled to the door and whispered, "I think they're outside the door."

They both looked toward the door and made a move to get up. Just then, the doorbell rang and they heard three voices yelping.

Tom jumped to his feet, saying, "They're standing between us and the food I organized for us."

He opened the library door and shook his head. Leaning forward, Evie saw the others rushing away from the library but, sensing him, they stopped.

"Tom," Henrietta exclaimed. "We didn't expect to find you here."

"Are you all retiring for the night?" Tom asked, his voice sounding hopeful.

"Oh, we hadn't really thought about it but now that you mention it, we might enjoy a nightcap. Yes, that would be a splendid idea. You're in the library, are you?"

When she saw Tom moving to block the door, Evie sighed and stood up.

"Henrietta, do come in and join us," she invited. "We are doing something extraordinary. Tom has organized a banquet for us prepared by The Criterion."

"Oh, a banquet." Henrietta looked at the others. "We had an early dinner but we'd love to join you."

"It's not exactly a banquet," Tom murmured.

"I suppose I should hunt down some plates and cutlery." Evie crossed the hall and was about to go into the dining room when the front door opened and Edgar walked in, clearly returning from his night at the theater.

He pointed to the door. "There is a chap outside, my lady. He is carrying a large basket. I'm sure he has the wrong address."

"No, he doesn't." Tom hurried to the door and took charge of the meal.

Henrietta sidled up to Edgar. "You might wish to assist her ladyship. She is about to raid your dinner service."

"No need to bother, Edgar," Evie said. "I can manage perfectly well."

Insisting, Edgar walked on through to the dining room and toward the butler's room beyond. "Where would you like me to set up, my lady?"

Sighing, Evie said, "We'll be in the library. The small table will do. We'll help ourselves."

That seemed to shock him. "I'll get a footman."

"Honestly, Edgar. There's no need to fuss. In fact, I insist." Turning, she saw Henrietta, Sara and Toodles holding a whispered conversation.

Toodles stepped forward. "Birdie, we just realized we came back early because we were tired. So, if you'll forgive us, we won't join you."

Evie could not have been more surprised. Earlier that day, instead of asking questions they had sat back and observed, and now, they were volunteering to give them time alone.

As they all made their way up the stairs, Evie turned and saw Tom disappearing inside the library. She stood alone in the hall for a moment murmuring, "This chaos is precisely what the new lady's maid would have to contend with."

Walking into the library, she saw two covered plates on the small table and Tom sitting by the fireplace taking a bite of something she couldn't quite make out.

"Where are the others?" he asked.

"They've excused themselves."

"Oh… I hope they didn't take exception to my remarks. I'm not even sure what I said. I suppose I'll have to apologize tomorrow."

"Never a dull moment," Evie murmured as she sat down. She picked up the piece of paper she had been writing on. Tapping her finger against it, she tried to pick up the trail of her thoughts.

"The detective said Merrin Smith was seen walking away from Mrs. Colliers' house. Did he say if she actually went to her house or did he assume she had?"

"The maid who telephoned the police must have seen her," Tom suggested.

She picked up the pen and scribbled a note. "We must find out how Mrs. Colliers died."

"And how do you propose wrenching the information out of the detective? I think you've run out of concessions."

Evie brushed her finger along her chin. "Not necessarily." She looked up at the ceiling.

That seemed to be all Tom needed to read her intentions. "You can't possibly be serious. You'd be prepared to use Caro to barter for information?"

"I'm sure she'd be a willing participant." Shrugging, she set the pen down again. "Of course, we could always rely on our resourcefulness. If reporters can obtain information that's been withheld, then we should be able to find a way…"

Tom snorted. "Extortion and bribery. What next? Open threats?"

Edgar walked in carrying a tray and busied himself setting the table for them. When he finished, he withdrew from the library only to return. Setting a candle stick in the middle of the table, he produced a box of matches and proceeded to light the candles.

Evie's eyes widened slightly. Whose idea had that been? Shaking her head, she asked, "Edgar, have you seen Millicent?"

"I believe she and Lady Evans were dining out tonight, my lady."

"Oh, marvelous. That means Millicent succeeded in cheering Caro up."

He inspected the contents in the tray and gave a nod of approval.

"We'll help ourselves, Edgar. Thank you."

He nodded. "I'll have some coffee brought up in an hour, my lady."

"That's very thoughtful. Thank you." Evie stood up and walked over to the table. Sitting down, she saw Tom remained sitting by the fireplace. "What's happened to your appetite?"

He looked distracted but joined her at the table. "I was just thinking we need to know more about Mrs. Colliers."

Another name to add to the list.

"She's obviously affluent," Evie mused as she served herself. "Appearances. We always seem to be led by outward appearances. How a person is dressed. Where they live. How they express themselves. How they occupy their time."

"And actions," Tom said. "I'm sure you have been somewhat swayed by Merrin Smith's refusal to reveal her employer's name and you've now formed solid opinions about her."

"Yes, I believe I felt she was protecting Lady Barton but it could have been nothing more than an attempt to keep her out of the limelight. Or… She might have been trying to buy some time and delay the inevitable."

"You think she wanted to give Lady Barton time? To do what?"

"That's a good question, but we're getting ahead of ourselves. It's best to maintain a steady course and collect information. That's what the police do."

"Not all the time. In this instance, they appear to have jumped to conclusions." Tom poured them each some wine. "A maid claimed Merrin Smith was responsible for killing Mrs. Colliers—"

"Did she?" Evie glanced over at her notes and tried to

recall what she'd written down. "I can't remember what the detective said."

Tom looked up. "He mentioned something about the maid contacting the police and naming Merrin Smith."

Evie nodded. "And she described her, so she must have seen her in the house." Evie hummed and wished they could know more. Had the maid panicked? Had her voice quivered? Had she cried? Or had she been matter-of-fact. "Yes, we need more information.

The clock struck the hour. A brief moment later, Edgar walked in and announced, "Lotte Mannering, my lady."

CHAPTER 10

The lady detective surprised them with her appearance and not just because they were not expecting her. Evie had never before seen Lotte dressed in formal attire. She looked resplendent in a midnight blue beaded evening gown. A master of disguise, Lotte had the ability to change her entire demeanor. Right then, she looked haughtier than the most pompous of duchesses.

Tom drew out a chair for her, his expression as impressed as Evie's.

"Please excuse my attire," Lotte offered in a soft, yet exaggerated cultured tone, "I've been trailing a hood-winker intent on defrauding a widow. I'm sure the Brooklyn Bridge is not for sale."

Edgar returned with an extra table setting for Lotte.

"Just coffee for me, thank you. Although, some brandy would not go amiss."

As Edgar poured her a brandy, Lotte rummaged through her silk purse and drew out a small notebook. She looked up for a moment and tilted her head in thought. "I believe I was propositioned by a much younger man, but then... one can't be sure these days. He might have been after my diamonds. I'm tempted to see how far it goes. I believe he stands to inherit a castle but has no means to pay for a new roof." She gave a whimsical smile. "My paste jewels might be enough to spring for some buckets."

She turned her attention to the notebook and turned several pages until she found the one she wanted. "The East India Club. That's where your man is staying. He went there straight from White's. I had one of my chaps, Freddy, follow him. Freddy made a special note about Wilfred Greer's leisurely gait. He walked there so Wilfred Greer is obviously not in any hurry." Lotte lowered her notebook and looked pensive. "Freddy also noted a strange incident at the East India Club. A man and a woman went in. They looked quite determined and must have had some business there." Lotte stopped and cast a scrutinizing glance at Tom and Evie who were still wearing their street clothes. "They were not dressed in evening clothes which suggests they might belong to a different social stratum."

Evie glanced at Tom and smiled. "Oh, I wonder what sort of business they had at the club."

"My man observed them sitting in a roadster outside the club." Lotte referred to her notebook. "A Duesenberg Straight Eight." Setting her notebook down, she looked toward the window facing the street. "Strange, I'm sure the motor I saw outside is a Duesenberg Straight Eight."

"Heavens, what a coincidence," Evie remarked nonchalantly. "Oh, do have some of this partridge. It's delectable."

Declining, Lotte gave her a look of admiration. "Going

to the gentlemen's club took more pluck than I ever gave you credit for."

Evie grinned. "Thank you. I must admit it felt rather exhilarating. It was quite daring and I'm surprised we didn't cause a scene."

Tom lowered his fork and knife and smiled at Evie. "I think you're more disappointed than surprised."

"May I ask what took you there?" Lotte asked.

Evie realized Lotte didn't know about their interest in a current case. She told her about holding the interviews and then reading about one of the candidates being questioned by the police.

"Anyhow, we went to the club to deliver a piece of information. Detective Inspector Evans is staying there. Imagine our surprise when we saw Wilfred Greer at the club."

"I see. You already knew of his presence there." Lotte frowned and picked up her brandy. Taking a pensive sip, she then said, "When your butler opened the door, he looked disappointed. When I questioned him, he explained he'd been expecting your maid, Millicent, and Lady Evans. Is she visiting?"

Evie nodded.

"And Detective Inspector Evans is staying at his club..."

Evie smiled. "It's a long story."

Tom raised his glass of wine. "There's never a dull moment here."

Agreeing, Evie added, "Here or at Halton House."

"Or wherever you might happen to be?" Lotte asked.

Evie glanced at Lotte. She recalled the time the lady detective had disguised herself as an indigent woman and had then pretended to be quite mad. "There are times when I feel my life imitates the most outrageous fictional tales. Anyhow, your timing could not have been more perfect. Tom and I were about to discuss strategy."

Tom's eyebrows lifted slightly. "We were?"

"Yes, remember we'd decided we needed to collect information and strategizing is the natural next step."

Grinning, Tom looked at Lotte. "Evie wants to use Lady Evans to extort information from her husband."

"Extort?" Lotte exclaimed. "I thought Detective Inspector Evans welcomed your input and was happy to share information with you."

Evie sighed. "Circumstances have changed. I'm afraid I've become rather a thorn in his side."

"Does this have something to do with Lady Evans' presence at Woodridge House?" Lotte asked.

Evie really didn't wish to discuss Caro's marital problems. Turning the focus of the conversation back to the case, she said, "If we can't rely on the detective sharing information with us, we'll need to become more resourceful."

Lotte nodded. "My current case only keeps me busy in the evenings. Otherwise, I'm quite free to assist."

"Oh, marvelous," Evie exclaimed. "Tom and I will welcome any help we can get. We have this business with Merrin Smith being questioned about Mrs. Colliers' murder."

Lotte took a sip of her drink. Setting the glass down, she tapped her finger against it. "Did you say Mrs. Colliers?"

"Yes," Evie confirmed. "She lives in Belgravia. Lyall Street."

Lotte took another sip of her brandy.

"Does the name sound familiar?" Evie asked.

"Ratchenko."

"Who's that?" Evie asked.

"Mrs. Colliers." Lotte's upper crust accent thickened and filled with distaste. "Her real name is Ratchenko. A Russian émigré of ill repute."

Evie tried to imagine what the woman had done to earn such a reputation, but failed. "What sort of ill repute?"

"Rumors about her abound. Not in well to-do circles but rather deep in the heart of the seedier parts of town. Some say she murdered her employer, a Russian Countess or maybe a Grand Duchess. They did so love to augment themselves. It's said Ratchenko worked as her housekeeper and, when the revolution came, she assisted her employer to flee the country. She only took her as far as the border. You see, the Grand Duchess had loaded herself up with all her jewels, sewing them into her clothes. Ratchenko used her as a mule and when she no longer had any use for her, she slit her throat and took the jewels, using the proceeds from the sale to establish herself in Belgravia as Mrs. Colliers."

Sitting back, Evie clutched her throat. "Heavens. That's quite a rumor."

Tom poured Evie another glass of wine. She took it and downed the contents.

"That's only one of the rumors floating around." Lotte tilted her head. "What was the other name?"

"Merrin Smith."

"Merrin Smith? Isn't she one of the young women your secretary engaged me to follow?"

Evie nodded. "Imagine my surprise when I saw her name plastered in the afternoon edition." Evie tried to remember what Lotte had reported. "The pub. According to you, she spent every night at the pub." She turned to Tom. "Of course, it makes sense now. We know Lady Barton has been relying on another lady's maid, and that's probably the reason why Merrin Smith was able to step out every night."

"She didn't appear to be having a good time of it," Lotte remarked.

"What do you mean?"

Lotte swirled the contents of her glass. "She fidgeted a great deal and kept looking over her shoulder."

"Perhaps she has a nervous disposition. I noticed she fidgeted during the interview."

"Or…" Tom shrugged. "She might have spent this last week making plans to murder Mrs. Colliers."

Evie couldn't explain the reasons for not believing her capable of murder. She just didn't.

"Logic tells me we should start with Merrin Smith and learn everything we can about her background but she's only ever worked for Lady Barton. Before coming to London, she lived in a small village near Brighton." Would they discover anything of interest if they spoke with the other servants employed by Lady Barton?

Edgar entered and set a tray with coffee and cups.

"Thank you, Edgar. I'll take it from here," Tom said. With their meals finished, Tom poured coffee into two cups and they settled by the fireplace.

Evie read through her notes. "Is there anyway of verifying those rumors about Mrs. Colliers?" She answered her own question with a nod. "Yes, of course. We could at least confirm where she came from. There would be traces of an accent. But would any of the servants have the ability to recognize it? To some people, a foreign accent is a foreign accent. Of course, there could be some sort of telltale sign in her house. Things such as religious icons. Or... a preference for vodka. Books written in Russian."

Lotte produced her notebook and took some notes. "Would you like me to look into it?"

"Do you think you can gain access to the servants?"

"That would be the easy part," Lotte said. "The hard part would be in getting them to say something worthwhile. They'll definitely talk. I have no doubt about that. Money is a great motivator."

Once they had some background information on Mrs. Colliers, they might focus on motive.

Why would someone want to kill her?

"It would help to know how she died," Evie mused. "The information could be quite revealing in itself."

"How so?" Tom asked.

Evie sighed. "Oh, dear. Sometimes, I speak without thinking." She looked up at the ceiling. "Let me see. Where could my thoughts have been going? Oh, yes. Crime of passion. Those sound rather gruesome and, I imagine, quite messy. If she had been stabbed in the drawing room with a letter opener, we could imagine someone argued with her, lost their temper and employed the first tool they could find. If the killer planned the murder, they might have used their own knife, hidden in a pocket or a handbag. It might suggest there had been some planning involved." Evie shrugged and sat back. "If she was struck with something, that might indicate a sudden burst of anger and need to act without thinking. Although, that's not written in stone. It could also be a random act of violence."

They knew a maid had telephoned the police to report the crime. Had she found the body or had she reacted to someone else raising the alarm? Had they described the scene to the police?

"Assuming the detective will not share this vital piece of information with us," Tom said. "What do you propose doing?"

Evie glanced at Lotte. "There is an informant working for the police, I'm sure of it. Someone leaked Merrin Smith's name to the newspaper."

Lotte steepled her fingers and drummed them together. "I'll get one of my boys to visit some of the local pubs near the police station."

Evie frowned. "If someone is selling information, wouldn't they do it in a place where other police officers wouldn't see them?"

"You're right and they might have established a meeting place and have a set of signals to suggest they have information."

"The barkeeper near the police station," Tom suggested. "He's bound to know something."

"Splendid idea, Tom. We might not even be looking for a policeman. It could just be a case of the barkeeper eavesdropping on conversations."

Encouraged by the progress they'd made, Evie turned her thoughts to Lady Barton. Would Henrietta or Sara know her? Could she risk asking them? Once she opened that particular door, she wouldn't be able to close it. They would definitely wish to know why she was asking.

"How does one ask questions about a particular person without stimulating curiosity?" she asked.

"By weaving the name into a conversation," Lotte suggested. Adopting her haughty voice, she said, "There I was trying on a pair of kid gloves, when a woman trod on my foot. She apologized and then had the temerity to introduce herself as if I would wish to become better acquainted with someone who had trampled on me. What was her name? Oh, yes, Lady Barton."

Evie clapped her hands. "Bravo! That was a fine performance, Lotte, but I'm not sure I'll have the courage to employ such a tactic with Henrietta. She's quite astute and she's already suspicious."

Tom laughed. "You might not want to try it, but Millicent would jump at the opportunity."

"You're right. I'll propose it to her tomorrow."

They spent the next hour familiarizing Lotte with the few facts they had accumulated. That meant covering the same ground, something Evie usually found helpful as she sometimes succeeded in detecting details they might have otherwise missed. But not so this time.

At the stroke of midnight, Lotte made a move to leave. "I'll organize one of my fellows to look into the police officer leaking information to the newspapers."

"Yes, that would be a good starting point." With any luck, Evie thought they might be able to gain insight into any new developments.

When Lotte also mentioned trying to talk with Mrs. Colliers' servants, Evie decided to relieve Lotte of the task.

"Is that a good idea, Countess?" Tom asked. He glanced at the clock as if to suggest there wouldn't be enough time to come up with a plan. "How do you propose going about it?"

"We'll figure something out tomorrow, Tom."

"What about Wilfred Greer?" Lotte asked. "Do you still want him followed?"

Evie looked at Tom. "What do you think? Has Henry set your mind at ease?"

"Not in the least. In fact, I'm more curious than ever," he said.

Tom walked Lotte to her motor car and returned to find Evie turning out lights.

"I'm sure Edgar has been waiting for his cue but I suspect he's fallen asleep," she said.

"Edmonds took care of the roadster so I'll take care of the fire and do the rounds of the house," he said.

Evie made her way up to her room. She needed a good night's rest and pondering unanswered questions would be a sure way to disrupt it, so she dismissed all thoughts from her mind.

However, as she drifted off to sleep, she found herself wondering about Mr. Colliers. "Is there a Mr. Colliers?"

CHAPTER 11

The next morning, Evie stirred awake and before she even opened her eyes, she exclaimed, "Millicent!"

And Caro...

Had they returned from their evening outing?

The previous night, she and Tom had been so involved in sorting out the day's events, she'd completely forgotten about Millicent and Caro.

What if something had happened to them?

Yelping, Evie flung the covers back, jumped out of bed and hurried toward her wardrobe only to collide with Millicent as she rushed into the bedroom.

"Milady!"

"Oh, heavens. Millicent. You gave me such a fright."

"I-I'm sorry. I was headed this way when I heard you yelp so I hurried in."

"That's not why you gave me a fright." Evie pressed her hand to her brow. "When did you come back?"

"From where, milady?"

"Last night. You and Caro went out."

Millicent nodded and smiled. "Caro... I mean, Lady Evans and I reveled in our freedom." Lowering her voice, she said, "We've never been to a jazz club. It all looked so dazzling and vibrant with everyone dancing and laughing and the music was marvelous."

Relieved to hear they had not come to any harm, she asked, "Did Caro really enjoy herself?"

"Oh, yes. She didn't want to leave. We were both asked to dance but we didn't know the steps. They look simple enough but I just didn't have the courage to even try."

"Will there be a next time?" Evie asked.

"To be perfectly honest, milady, I don't know what's going through Caro's mind. When I asked how long she'd be staying, she almost wept. So I thought it best not to mention it again."

As she spoke, Caro moved about the room collecting the clothes Evie had worn the previous day. She put them away in the wardrobe and selected fresh clothes for that day.

"Will you be going out today, milady?"

"Yes. Most likely. Oh, I just remembered the last thought I had last night." She walked over to her bedside table, picked up her notebook and sat down on the edge of the bed to write a note to herself. "Mr. Colliers. We need to find out if he exists."

"I'll draw you a bath, milady." Walking toward the boudoir, Millicent asked, "Did you and Mr. Winchester have any success yesterday?"

"I'm not sure, Millicent." She proceeded to tell her about everything they had found out the previous day, including Lotte's visit.

"I feel I should be writing all this down, milady."

"That won't be necessary, Millicent. I've been taking notes. We have question marks next to a couple of names. I'm sure once we know more about Lady Barton and Mrs. Colliers, we'll be able to make some sort of connection. Today, we are going to try to speak with Mrs. Colliers' servants."

"Didn't you say Lotte Mannering would be organizing one of her chaps to do that?"

"Oh, yes. However, just before Lotte left, I suggested Tom and I should undertake that task."

"And how did you find Lord Evans? Was he in good spirits?"

Evie gave it some thought. "I wouldn't say he was overjoyed to see us. However, I'm sure he appreciated the information we gave him."

Bathed and dressed, Evie sat at her dresser and picked up a bottle of scent. She inhaled its flowery scent and smiled.

"What can we do?" Millicent asked.

"We?"

"Lady Evans and I."

"Oh, heavens. I couldn't really ask Caro to become involved."

"It might be the best thing for her, milady. She's eager to keep busy."

"I'm sure she is, but I'm eager to stay on the right side of Detective Inspector Evans. Perhaps you could visit a museum." Evie's eyes brightened. "Or, you could actually do me a favor and make sure Henrietta and the others are kept busy."

Smiling, Millicent agreed. "That should keep us on our toes."

Evie glanced at her mirror and saw Millicent studying the handle on a handbag. "Is something the matter, Millicent?"

Looking up, Millicent gave her a worried look. "I was just wondering how you were going to approach Mrs. Colliers' servants. I feel this is something I should be involved in."

"You're right, but remember we are more concerned about Caro and keeping her away from the investigation. Mr. Winchester and I will find a way. Lotte proposed taking care of it herself and using money as an incentive, but she is already looking into the police officer leaking information. I'm sure that will work for us too." Evie knew it would have been more expedient to rely on one of Lotte's men. However, barging inside one of London's most exclusive gentlemen's club had given her a taste of excitement. "I am determined to give it my best, Millicent. Without the detective's cooperation, I fear we will have to rely on our creativity."

She inspected herself in the mirror and complimented Millicent on her choice of clothes.

"I put in some extra effort, milady."

Millicent didn't need to explain herself. With Caro's presence came a desire to impress.

Evie smiled. "I know Caro will approve. If she doesn't, I will simply tell her I imposed my own poor taste on you." She looked for her little black notebook and slipped it inside her pocket.

Millicent's eyes widened slightly, prompting Evie to say, "I should keep it handy, just in case. Remember, all this started with me seeing the headline in the newspaper. Heaven only knows what sort of news awaits me this morning. Whatever happens, I need to keep track of it all."

Evie walked out of her room, a spring in her step, which she kept up as she went downstairs. However, when she neared the morning room, her steps slowed.

She never knew who would be sitting down to breakfast.

A footman emerged from the morning room carrying an empty tray. Seeing her, he nodded and stepped aside to let Evie through.

"Good morning, Jon." Lowering her voice, she asked, "Who's in there?"

"Mr. Winchester, my lady. The ladies Henrietta and Sara and Toodles have all asked for breakfast to be taken up."

Evie's eyebrows rose a notch. She thanked him and walked in to find Tom reading the morning newspaper.

Lowering it, he glanced over her shoulder.

"No, there's no one following me in." Evie helped herself to breakfast and sat down opposite Tom. "I can hardly believe it. The others are not coming down to breakfast. What do you think it means? They've never given us such a wide berth."

"Are you complaining?"

"I feel I should say I'm merely curious but I'm actually suspicious. What could they be up to?"

She buttered a piece of toast. Setting her knife down, she stared straight ahead, so lost in her thoughts, she didn't even realize she was looking straight at Tom.

The edge of Tom's lip lifted. "I'm sure you'll eventually tell me."

It took Evie a moment to respond. "Lady Barton, Merrin Smith, Mrs. Colliers and Wilfred Greer. To some, they might sound like random names. We know there is a small connection because Merrin Smith works for Lady Barton and she's been questioned by the police in regards to Mrs. Colliers' murder. But what if there is a stronger connection?"

"That's possible but how is Wilfred Greer connected?"

"Coincidence. Remember, we don't really like or even believe in coincidences. Now, more than ever, I'm inclined to think there's a reason why you noticed him when you did and why we saw him at the club."

"I won't disagree because, if I do, you will no doubt prove me wrong." Tom drained his coffee and got up to pour himself another cup.

"Have you given any thought to how we'll approach Mrs. Colliers' servants?" Tom asked. "I've been racking my brain and I haven't come up with anything."

She'd hoped to wake up with a bright idea ready to execute. Now, they would have to rely on inspiration. "I know you objected to the change of plans but I'm sure we'll find a way."

Instead of returning to the table, he went to stand by the window facing the street.

"Are you checking to see if we are being watched?" She couldn't think of any other reason why he would be drawn to the view.

"As you suggested, seeing Wilfred Greer might not have been a coincidence," Tom said and returned to the table. Seeing her frowning, he offered an assurance, "I'm sure there's no need to worry."

Evie gave him a brisk smile. "I hope that's not your

way of shielding me." Tom had tried that tactic once before, justifying it by saying he hadn't wanted her to worry unnecessarily. But that had been in the early days of their... Evie searched for the right definition. After a moment, she decided they had a partnership, with complimentary talents. Yes, indeed. A solid relationship.

She took a sip of her coffee and looked at the clock on the mantle. "It might be a good idea to ask Edmonds to bring the roadster around. We should head to Mrs. Colliers' house as soon as we've finished breakfast." Evie shrugged. "I'm sure if we're patient enough, one of the servants will step out of the house this morning and we'll be able to approach them."

Tom lifted an eyebrow but didn't comment.

"Do you have a better idea?" Evie asked.

"No, but I'm surprised you're willing to sit around and wait for something to happen."

What else could they do?

Go in, guns blazing? She only wanted to speak with the servants. Other than the rumor connected to Mrs. Colliers, she knew next to nothing about her.

Someone had killed her and they must have had a very good reason for it. Servants had the advantage of hearing and seeing everything. Someone must have noticed something strange happening in Mrs. Colliers' life.

"I wish there was some way of finding out what the detective has discovered."

Merrin Smith remained in prison. The detective must have found something to point the finger at her. Could they ask to see her?

"I believe we have our work cut out for us."

Heavens. They still didn't know how Mrs. Colliers died.

Evie groaned. "I really need to refer to my notes. I should have asked Lotte to look into it."

"Look into what? Countess, you can't start a conversation without a reference to the subject."

Grinning, Evie apologized. "Mrs. Colliers' death. I know I keep harping on about it, but the fact remains, we simply don't know and that should have been one of our first questions. The answer could be quite revealing." Her eyes brightened. "Oh, we could pretend to be friends who know nothing about her death."

Tom shook his head. "I'm still in the dark. Sometimes, your ideas are like floodwaters. They spread into several tributaries and head in all directions."

Evie held up a finger. "At the risk of repeating myself, we still need to find out how Mrs. Colliers died." Holding up another finger, she said, "We also wish to speak with her servants. I wonder if we could walk right up to the front door and pretend we don't know anything about her death…"

Tom nodded. "I'm all caught up now." He finished his coffee and, sitting back, he drummed his fingers on the table.

Interpreting the gesture as impatience, Evie said, "Instead of waiting around for something to happen, I thought you'd appreciate a more direct approach."

He stood up. "I'll get the roadster."

"And I'll fetch my coat." Evie followed him out of the morning room.

Walking up the stairs, Evie heard Tom say, "I guess there's no need."

She turned, looked down and saw Tom standing by the front door.

"Edmonds is outside polishing the roadster." He walked toward the stairs and stopped when Edgar appeared, a silver salver in hand.

"This arrived for you, Mr. Winchester."

Thanking him, Tom took the letter and turned the envelope in his hands. His eyes widened ever so slightly. Tucking the envelope inside his pocket, he caught up with Evie.

She wanted to ask him about the missive but decided to leave it up to him to reveal its contents, when and if he saw fit.

Hurrying up the stairs, Evie said, "I'll meet you downstairs in a moment."

In her room, she went through the contents of her handbag, making sure she had everything she needed. She put on her coat and hat and picked up her gloves as she whispered, "Detective Inspector O'Neil." She could telephone him, but would he share information with her? She imagined he had heard about the case and he'd come to trust her instincts, such as they were. Walking out of her room, she thought about that. The lack of factual information limited her abilities. She couldn't make something up out of nothing.

Realizing Lord Evans would not appreciate her going over his head, she dismissed the idea.

When she reached the bottom of the stairs, she stopped.

Tom stood by the door waiting for her. She looked at him, her expression as blank as her mind. "Remind me again why we're doing this."

He put his hat on and smiled. "We believe Merrin Smith sent you an open invitation to assist her."

Her brows furrowed. "We do?"

Tom nodded.

Scratching around her mind, she remembered reaching that conclusion. Merrin Smith had refused to give out the name of her employer but had volunteered her name.

"Would you believe I'd forgotten all about that."

Tom gave her an encouraging smile. "Are you ready or have you had a change of mind?"

"I'm ready." She crossed the hall. "Where's Holmes?"

"Edgar only just left with him. They're headed for the park for Holmes' constitutional."

"I'm glad someone's taking care of him. Honestly, I don't know where my mind is this morning." If she had to be honest, she'd never felt so indecisive.

Evie scooped in a deep breath.

The night before, she had fallen asleep wondering if there was a Mr. Colliers in the scene and, that morning, she had woken up yelping Millicent's name because she had forgotten to see if she had returned from her outing.

Tom held the door open for her. They stepped out of Woodridge House, their eyes on the roadster, or so it seemed.

As they walked toward the roadster, their gazes slanted and they surveyed the street.

Evie knew Tom had always taken such a precaution. When had she started doing it?

They both looked to the right and to the left and to the right again.

"Is it my imagination?" Evie asked.

Tom shook his head. "I don't think so."

"So you noticed it?"

Tom held the passenger door open. "Indeed, I did. I've never seen that motor car in this street. It doesn't look new so it can't be a new acquisition by one of the neighbors. Also, the motor is running."

Someone was ready to follow them…

CHAPTER 12

"What do you propose doing?" she asked.

Tom rounded the roadster and took his place at the driver's seat. "Well, I can only think of one suggestion. We drive and see if they follows us."

Evie nodded and settled into her seat. "Tally-ho!" The barrage of thoughts she'd been entertaining were all pushed aside. While Evie kept her attention on the street ahead, she battled against the urge to look over her shoulder.

Tom drove at a sedate pace. Crossing the first intersection, he then stepped on the gas and accelerated.

"Are they keeping up?" Evie asked.

"Yes."

When he slowed down, they slowed down. Always keeping a safe distance.

There were only a couple of other motor cars on the road but as they headed away from Woodridge House they encountered more vehicles.

"Still there?" she asked.

"Yes." Tom made a turn and drove for a couple of blocks.

When he made another turn, Evie glanced back and saw the motor behind them and still keeping a discreet distance.

Who could possibly be following them and why? Evie knew the same questions were running through Tom's mind.

"Countess, I'm going to stop soon."

"Do you have a plan?"

"I want you to remain vigilant. If anyone comes near you, head inside that pub," he said and signaled to the pub at the end of the street. He reached down. When he straightened, he put something rather heavy on her lap and told her the rest of his plan.

"Oh, heavens."

"I know you can use one of those."

Yes, indeed. Ever since she'd been able to hold one. Although, she'd never been as keen as her brother who'd enjoyed hunting rabbits and had been instrumental in teaching her how to use a gun. She wrapped her fingers around the revolver and nodded.

Following Tom's train of thought, she knew he was taking care of all possibilities.

The moment he stepped out of the roadster, she'd be left alone. What if someone wanted to separate them?

After a spate of kidnappings back home, Toodles had taken the precaution of engaging Tom as her bodyguard. No matter where their relationship took them, he would always remain her bodyguard.

"When I stop, I'm going to walk down the street and pretend I'm looking for an address."

"And then you're going to double back and catch them by surprise?" she asked.

"Precisely."

Evie dug inside her handbag and produced a small compact mirror. "I'm ready."

Tom maneuvered the motor into an empty space. They both made a point of looking up and down the street. Evie pointed at one building and then the other, doing her best to pretend they were looking for an address.

"They've stopped," Tom murmured and made a move to climb out of the roadster.

"Tom."

"Yes?"

She was the Countess of Woodridge. People in her position did not make public declarations. "Be careful, my love."

Taking a deep swallow, he smiled. "I will, my love." With a nod, he emerged from the roadster and walked at a steady pace, his attention on the buildings while, Evie guessed, his eyes remained slanted toward the other vehicle.

There were a few passersby. They glanced at Evie but continued on their way.

Evie held up the compact mirror and positioned it so she could keep track of Tom without giving herself away. Tilting it, she brought the other vehicle into view.

Tom continued walking, at one point, stopping to look up the number on the building before continuing on.

That's when Evie decided to act as a decoy. If the person in the other vehicle had their attention fixed on Tom, she would distract them.

Shifting in her seat, she glanced one way and then the other and even made a move to step out of the roadster. "Yes, that's right. Look at me." She slipped the revolver inside her pocket. When she saw Tom had reached the end of the street, Evie stepped out of the roadster and stood beside it, her fingers curled around the revolver handle, ready to offer whatever assistance she could. That had not been part of Tom's plan but he'd have to learn to live with her inspired actions.

Tom doubled back, reached the vehicle and caught the person by surprise. The man swiveled in his seat and gaped at him, a sign he had been watching Evie.

When she saw Tom step away from the vehicle, her fingers curled tighter around the revolver.

A man stepped out of the motor car and tipped his hat back. Dressed in a gray suit with no distinguishing features, he looked to be about the same height as Tom, perhaps slightly shorter, Evie thought.

Evie searched for signs of aggression and frowned when she saw Tom smiling.

The two men turned and headed toward Evie.

"What is going on?" she murmured under her breath.

When they reached her, Tom made the introductions, using her maiden name instead of her title. "Evie Parker, this is James Peters, he's a journalist."

"Evie Parker?" the journalist asked.

"If you want to talk to us, you will have to agree to addressing her ladyship as Evie Parker."

To maintain her privacy, she guessed.

"What's this about, Tom?" Evie asked.

"Do you remember that theory you had about a policeman selling information to a journalist? Well, this is the journalist purchasing the information. Of course, he refuses to identify his source but, at the same time, he has not denied having a police informant."

The journalist drew in a deep breath. "I guess I let that one slip."

"Anyhow," Tom continued, "James Peters has come into more information. He knows Merrin Smith mentioned your name to the police. He is also aware of the fact you are the Countess of Woodridge, the very one who enjoys dabbling in mysteries. So, our intrepid friend decided to follow you to see if you would lead him somewhere interesting."

Intrepid friend?

"Are we now collaborating with him?" Evie asked. It actually seemed like a very good idea, especially if it came with a caveat to keep her name out of the newspaper.

Tom nodded. "If you agree to it, yes."

Evie couldn't see why they shouldn't take advantage of the offer. They'd wanted to identify the police officer selling information so they could avail themselves of his services. Now they could simply work through James Peters.

Gesturing toward the pub, Tom said, "Shall we go in and sit down for a moment?"

Evie glanced at her wristwatch. "The pub hasn't opened yet." She looked down the street and saw a small tea room. Drawing in a deep breath, she suggested, "A brief chat and a cup of tea?"

CHAPTER 13

*E*vie had no idea what to make of the journalist. As she sat opposite him, she decided to give him the benefit of the doubt and hear him out. Although, she couldn't help entertaining a few reservations.

After all, he had followed them. Indeed, he had actually stalked her and waited near her home.

Reason told her she might have done the same but Evie didn't wish to listen to reason.

They placed an order for tea. When the waitress walked away, Evie said, "I understand how you found out my name, but how did you find my address? I met Merrin Smith in a pub, not at my home."

James Peters nodded in understanding. "Merrin Smith told the police she answered an advertisement in an agency."

"And you obtained this information through your informant."

He nodded. "I engaged the assistance of a female colleague. She went to the agency and applied for a job."

Evie frowned. "But the agency has not been giving out my address because the interviews have been held at a pub."

Smiling, he explained, "My colleague distracted the person interviewing her and looked for the address."

How very resourceful, Evie thought. "What guarantee do I have you'll keep my name out of the newspaper?"

"I believe we could all benefit from an ongoing association. I have my sources and you have your abilities and talents."

Evie smiled at his attempt to flatter her. Of course, his proposal sounded like a fair exchange and she rather relished the idea of having another contact in the know.

She glanced at Tom and was surprised to see him nod in approval.

"Very well. As a show of faith—"

"Of course," he hurried to say. Leaning forward, he lowered his voice. "The police don't actually have any proof of wrongdoing. Nothing to suggest Merrin Smith is the killer. No motive. No weapon. Nothing."

That came as a shock. "So why are they holding her?"

He gave a brisk nod. "The maid who telephoned the police said Merrin Smith came to the house. She assumed she had an appointment. She met with the owner of the house. They had a brief meeting behind closed doors and then Merrin Smith rushed out of the house."

"You obtained this information directly from the police contact?" Tom asked.

"Yes."

Their tea arrived and they went through the motions of pouring and sipping.

If the police claimed they hadn't found a motive,

then they must have established the fact Merrin Smith had never had anything to do with Mrs. Colliers. Why would they continue holding her? What proof did the maid provide to confirm Merrin Smith had been at the house?

"Do you know how she died?" Evie asked.

"My man thinks it was a stab wound."

Evie's eyebrows lowered. "He's not sure?"

"The detective in charge is eager to keep as much information as possible under wraps. He's not pleased about the suspect's name being leaked and has threatened everyone with severe repercussions if they so much as breathe a word about the case. My informant only found out the suspect's name, because he was there when the police brought her in for questioning. His shift ended soon after. He picked up some other bits and pieces from other officers, but nothing significant."

"And that's when he provided you with the name?" Evie asked.

James Peters nodded and continued, "I managed to get the article into the next edition. By the time my informant returned to work the next day, the embargo on information had been imposed."

And now he was as much in the dark as they were...

"It seems our fair exchange of information has hit a wall," Evie mused.

"I have a wide net of connections, people who turn their attention to what's being said and done," he assured her. "They are quite willing to observe and report."

Evie nodded. "It's just a matter of you knowing where to direct them to."

"Precisely."

Evie sighed. "We were on our way to Mrs. Colliers' house. I suppose there'll be a police presence."

He shook his head. "They're strained as it is. They have already collected all the information they need."

Evie's eyebrows curved up. "That can't be right. They don't have a motive. Then again, they might have information they don't know what to do with or how to interpret."

Evie picked up her teaspoon and twirled it about. "We need to speak with the maid who placed the telephone call, the one who told the police she saw Merrin Smith."

"How do you plan on doing that?" James Peters asked.

They hadn't thought that far ahead. "We were probably going to wait until one of the servants stepped out of the house. We also had the idea of pretending to be Mrs. Colliers' friends and simply dropping by unannounced."

"I could try to see if one of the servants is willing to give a statement," he suggested.

"I'm surprised you haven't already tried that."

He looked down at his hands. "I only just found out the name of the victim."

And she'd given him that information!

The detective must have really tightened his grip on the investigation.

"Since you know the name of the victim, I assume you also know the address," he said. "How did you manage that?"

Evie thought back to the moment the detective had referred to his notes and given her the full address. She only now realized how generous he had been to divulge the information.

Had it been a deliberate attempt to draw her into the

investigation? That, Evie thought, would be quite ironic. On the one hand, he didn't want Caro becoming involved, while at the same time he was prepared to share vital information, luring Evie into carrying out her own inquiries.

"We have our own reliable sources," Evie said.

"I'm impressed."

She realized that might be a way to establish trust. He had his sources and they had theirs.

Dipping her head, Evie smiled. She had no idea how long her source of information would be willing to play along. For all she knew, they'd already exhausted all their concessions.

"Very well. Tom and I will lead the way and I'm sure you won't have any trouble following us."

They returned to their respective motor cars.

"Countess? Why do I feel you're not entirely pleased with the arrangement?"

Perhaps because she wasn't. Tom's ability to interpret her silences still managed to surprise her. Although, she had to admit, she actually found it quite comforting. Then again, she didn't always wish to be read like an open book.

"Why did you think I would want James Peters to join us?"

"I'm not sure I understand what you mean."

"When you sneaked up on him, I expected you to send him on his way."

"Really? Are you saying you weren't the least bit interested in meeting a reporter who'd been following us?"

"That's just it. He'd been following us."

Tom checked for traffic and then pulled away. "So, in your opinion, that warranted some sort of punishment?"

Tom shook his head. "You wanted me to deliver some sort of harsh reprimand. Or perhaps you wanted me to brandish my revolver."

"Mock me all you want, Mr. Winchester. Only yesterday you'd been prepared to give Lord Evans a good horse whipping."

"And you discouraged me. Are you saying there are different rules for different people?"

"Not at all. I'm... I'm worried we might be trusting the wrong person and, admittedly, I'm also thinking about Caro and, in particular, Henry's warning. Actually, I'm also thinking of myself. Or, rather, the Woodridge family name. You know I've always been wary of bringing it into disrepute."

"I doubt James Peters will have a reason to include Caro's name in an article or even yours. Just in case, we could make it a condition."

"What if it's some sort of scoop and he can't resist?"

"Then I'll give him a good horse whipping."

Evie sighed. "Now I know you're mocking me." Evie knew Tom preferred a quiet and subtle approach. "You should at least show him your holstered revolver. You do still carry it?"

He nodded. "That reminds me..." He stretched his hand out.

Evie patted her pocket. "I think I'll keep it. Thank you."

Tom glanced at her and frowned. "Should I be worried?" He answered his own question by saying, "You're right. We should find out more about James Peters."

Evie sighed. "If you must know, I thought it was a

good idea to have him join us but then I didn't and now I'm not so sure."

Tom laughed. "Yes, no and maybe."

"As soon as this is over, I think we should both go away somewhere with fresh air and no one around to drag us into their troubles." She looked over her shoulder and then straightened. "He's right behind us. Now that he has us in his hook, he won't want to release us."

"Did you just use a fishing metaphor?"

"I believe I did."

They reached Lyall Street. She saw a maid sweeping the front steps of a house and another one polishing a doorknob. A chauffeur held a door open and a woman wearing a fur lined coat stepped in. Tom turned into the next street and stopped near the corner.

"We can see the house from here," he said.

James Peters followed them and stopped behind them. Evie watched him emerge from his motor car and pat his pockets as if to make sure he had what he needed.

He stopped by the roadster to ask, "Any last-minute instructions?"

Evie couldn't think of anything. "Oh, I'd like to know who else was in the house. I'm sure there's more than one maid and remember to ask about Mr. Colliers."

He tipped his hat and walked off in the direction of the house. Just as he crossed the street, a taxi cab drove up and stopped in the opposite corner.

Several other motor cars drove by blocking the taxi cab from view.

"Is someone getting out of the taxi cab?" Evie asked.

"I'm actually keeping my eye on James."

Evie looked away from the taxi cab and toward James

at the same time as Tom tore his attention away from James and looked at the taxi cab.

"It's pulling away," he said.

"James is standing at the door of the house," Evie reported.

"Oh."

"Oh?" Evie looked away from James. "What's happened?"

Tom leaned forward. "Is that…?"

"Yes, I believe it is."

Wilfred Greer.

He stood on the opposite corner and, she assumed, he had just climbed out of the taxi cab.

Evie saw him slip something inside his pocket. When he looked up, he stared straight ahead and toward Lyall Street. She watched him take a step and suddenly stop.

Tom and Evie turned toward Mrs. Colliers' house in time to see James turning away from the front door. Before walking down the steps, he glanced back and appeared to nod.

"Oh, dear. Does that mean she refused to speak with him? Did someone answer the door? I'm afraid I was looking away."

"I'm sorry, I didn't notice. I was looking at Wilfred Greer."

Glancing at the street corner, Evie's eyebrows hitched up. "Did Wilfred Greer stop because he saw James Peters?"

Tom gave a slow shake of his head. "I'm still puzzling over his presence here. However, I think you might be right. He's either surprised to see James Peters or he's intrigued by someone going to that address."

They both stared at him, waiting to see what he would do next.

"Heavens. Even from a distance I can see he's following James Peters' progress." The reporter was heading straight for them.

Evie lowered herself in her seat and saw Tom doing the same.

James Peters stopped by the roadster and peered down at them.

"Don't look around," Evie warned.

Too late. He looked up and across the street.

To his credit, he turned away. "Is that someone you know?" He shook his head as if suddenly losing interest. "The maid agreed to talk with me. She wants to meet at Eaton Square, the southern end." He tipped his hat and continued on to his vehicle.

When they heard him start his motor, Tom sat up, flicked the ignition switch, pulled the choke and flicked the clutch on the Duesenberg.

Evie tried to follow the sequence but her attention kept shifting to Wilfred Greer.

"He's not even pretending."

"No, he's looking straight at us." Tom drew in a breath and hissed it out.

"What's wrong? Why aren't we moving."

"I assume the maid is going to walk across to the square. What if Wilfred Greer is here to speak with her? He'll intercept her."

"What? Oh, heavens. I was happy to believe this was a coincidence."

Tom shook his head. "I don't believe it is."

A vehicle drove by, followed by another.

Wilfred Greer turned and looked down the street.

"I think he might be looking for a taxi cab."

"I doubt he'll have any luck. This is not exactly a main thoroughfare."

"Well, he's either waiting for someone or he is looking for a taxi cab. Either way, why on earth did he come here?"

They both gaped.

Wilfred Greer turned and began walking along Lyall Street, heading away from Mrs. Colliers' house.

"Good heavens."

"You sound affronted, Countess."

"And I feel it. Can we trust him to keep walking?" Evie asked.

Tom pointed toward the house. "She's coming out."

Evie straightened in her seat. "Wilfred Greer is coming back." He crossed the street at a steady clip, his attention speared straight ahead.

"He's going to intercept her," Evie said as the roadster jolted into motion. "Are you going to cut him off?"

Before Tom could respond, a motor car sped by and made a sharp turn into Lyall street, stopping abruptly in front of Mrs. Colliers' house.

Evie gasped. "Is that James Peters?"

The passenger door swung open and the maid hurried inside. Before she could secure the door shut, the motor car took off.

"Tom!"

Tom growled and sped after the car, making a sharp turn into Lyall street.

"Has he just abducted the maid?" she asked as she

swiveled back to see Wilfred Greer stop and gape at the speeding motor cars.

"He'll tell us soon enough when I catch up with him," Tom growled.

The roadster roared along Lyall street. Tom's knuckles showed white as he gripped the steering wheel.

"Don't lose him," Evie warned.

"Countess. I take exception to that. This is a Duesenberg Straight Eight. It has a racing engine."

"Yes, but this is not a racing track."

A horn blared as they raced across an intersection and made another sharp turn.

Belatedly, Tom called out, "Hold on."

Evie caught her breath. "Don't you worry about that. I'm holding on and I have no intention of letting go." In the next breath, she yelped.

"Now what?" Tom demanded.

Evie was looking over her shoulder. Straightening, she stammered, "I... I think I just saw the Duesenberg."

"Edmonds?"

She nodded.

"Was he alone?"

"I... I don't think so."

"Maybe it was just a coincidence."

"Heavens. I don't think I can take another one of those."

Keeping his eye on the road and the fleeing reporter, Tom growled. "Where's he headed? This is not the way to Eaton Square."

The reporter didn't show any sign of slowing down, but Tom didn't let him out of his sight.

James Peters made one turn after the other, avoiding

the main roads with their heavier traffic. Finally, he slowed down and, to Evie's relief, he thrust his arm out and pointed ahead.

Evie craned her neck. Ahead, she could see an explosion of greenery. "I think he's signaling to Hyde Park."

She sat back, crossed her arms and firmed her lips. "That was quite a stunt he pulled. I don't know what to make of it all. He might have mentioned something."

Tom scowled. "You're right. He should have said something."

Evie wanted to consider the possibility he had acted on the spur of the moment but she didn't feel inclined to make up excuses for him. "He'd better have a good explanation."

The reporter drove at a sedate pace now. It almost made her think he had been trying to put a safe distance between them and Mrs. Colliers' house.

If Tom had formed any opinions, he was keeping them to himself. Evie imagined they included several colorful words.

James Peters stopped near the corner opposite Hyde Park and emerged from the motor car. He leaned in and spoke to his passenger. With a nod, he rounded the vehicle and opened the passenger door.

The maid stepped out and pushed her coat collar up. She did not look at all pleased.

When Tom stopped the car, he sat back and pushed out a hard breath. "Let's take a moment to calm down," he suggested.

Evie lifted her chin. "I prefer to remain angry. While I place my full trust in your driving skills, I don't care to tempt fate."

Tom climbed out of the roadster first but Evie didn't wait for him to open the passenger door. She simply felt too impatient.

They walked with purpose, neither one speaking until they reached the couple.

James Peters had the nerve to greet them with a smile. "This is Daisy Wells. Miss Wells was eager to get as far away from the house as possible."

That was not what he'd originally told them.

While still smiling, the reporter looked contrite. "That was not premeditated." He lowered his voice and said, "As I drove away, I thought about that man you both appeared to be hiding from. Something about him looked familiar."

That caught their attention.

"I couldn't put my finger on it and I still can't. For some reason, he looked both suspicious and familiar. I only saw two other people walking along Lyall Street and they seemed to be heading somewhere. He wasn't. Anyhow, I decided to turn around thinking that if I was quick enough, I'd be able to get back in time to collect Miss Wells. Just in case…"

Evie swallowed. Could they trust him? Indeed. Could they believe his story?

CHAPTER 14

Hyde Park

The reporter and Miss Wells led the way across the busy street with Tom and Evie following several steps behind.

A glance from Tom prompted Evie to shrug as she interpreted his look. "I don't know. I really don't know if we can believe him. He sped away. We both saw it. Yes, he finally stopped but what if he realized he couldn't make his getaway?" She stopped long enough to draw in a breath. "We don't know what his intentions were…"

"I sense a however coming," Tom said.

"Yes. I can actually picture James Peters driving away to reach the rendezvous point, the image of Wilfred Greer in his mind, teasing and prodding his memory. He recognized a possible threat and turned back."

Waiting for a break in traffic, Tom cupped her elbow and they hurried across the street.

"At least we'll be able to lose ourselves in the crowd," Evie mused.

Even if Wilfred Greer managed to track them down to the park, he would have a hard time finding them. Traffic was heavier and there were more people.

They walked for about five minutes and finally stopped by a park bench. The reporter made the introductions. Miss Wells sat down and Evie joined her while Tom and the reporter stood in front of them.

Evie couldn't determine if the moment felt tense or filled with anticipation. Whatever they were about to hear would either provide them with clarity or puzzlement.

Miss Wells surprised her by speaking first, her words were measured and calm. "Mr. Peters said you were interested in learning about the events that took place yesterday." Daisy Wells' voice hitched. "All I can tell you is that Merrin Smith waltzed right in to Mrs. Colliers' house and slashed her throat from ear to ear."

Evie just barely stopped herself from gasping at the blunt statement.

"I've never seen anything so ghastly," Daisy Wells continued. "I don't mind telling you, I had to rush out and find a receptacle before I lost my lunch right there on Mrs. Colliers' expensive rug. Blood everywhere, there was, and I couldn't look away."

Throat slashed?

Despite her reaction, Evie struggled to imagine the violent scene. She just couldn't picture it because she couldn't see Merrin Smith doing something so violent.

Even after their brief encounter, the young woman just didn't seem capable of it.

"Who actually let Miss Smith in?" Tom asked.

"One of the maids. We don't have a butler. Only girls worked for Mrs. Colliers."

Evie produced her small notebook. "And what is the maid's name?"

Miss Wells firmed her lips. "I don't really want to say because that would be telling, wouldn't it?"

"But you won't be implicating her. We only wish to know where people were at the time of the incident." Evie looked up at Tom.

He gave an encouraging nod and said, "This is information we can obtain from the police but we want to hear your version of events."

That seemed to convince the young woman.

"It was Sofia."

"Would you mind spelling the name for me, please," Evie asked.

"It's written how it's sounded."

"Yes, but there are several ways of spelling it."

The maid thought about it and then spelled out the name.

To Evie, that sounded like a Russian version of Sophia. Perhaps that maid could confirm Mrs. Colliers' background.

"It is our understanding you saw Miss Smith leave the house in a rush."

Miss Wells nodded. "Yes, that's what happened. Just as I told the police."

"And how soon after Miss Smith left did you find Mrs. Colliers?"

The maid was about to answer but then stopped herself.

"Straightaway?" Evie prodded.

"N-no. Let me think... I had been tidying up the dining room. Mrs. Colliers had lunch promptly at midday and there was going to be a dinner party that night."

"While you were doing that, did you hear anything unusual?"

"What do you mean?"

"A sudden thump or a hard knock. Raised voices. Anything that might have sounded out of place."

"There's nothing unusual about those sounds. Mrs. Colliers' house was always noisy with people coming and going," Daisy explained.

"What sort of people?"

Miss Wells shrugged. "Mrs. Colliers was a social person. People always stopped by to pay her a visit."

"Men or women?" Evie asked.

The maid's cheeks flushed slightly. "Usually men."

"And where did she receive them?"

"In the library."

Not the drawing room? Why would Mrs. Colliers have her visitors shown through to the library? To Evie, that sounded like business, not pleasure.

"Is there a Mr. Colliers?" she asked.

"She told everyone there was but we never saw him and it wasn't our place to question her. If she said there was, then... there was one, tucked away somewhere." She bit the edge of her lip.

"What is it?" Evie prompted.

"When I said it was mostly men who came to see her... Well, in actual fact, once a week, usually on Fridays, young women came to see her." She tilted her head slightly. "If you ask me, they looked too proper."

"What do you mean?" Evie asked.

Miss Wells shrugged. "Like they were trying too hard. Proper but not really proper."

"How were they dressed?"

"In the height of fashion. Like you."

"So what made you think they were not entirely proper?"

Daily Wells tapped her fingers on her lap. "You can always tell, it's just difficult to put a finger on it. You know, there's just something off, something not quite right… Tawdry. Yes, that's the word. But it might be in the way they walked or that extra bit of rouge on their cheeks." She gave a firm nod. "Tawdry."

"And did those women stay long?" Tom asked.

"No. Maybe ten minutes or so."

Brief visits. That sounded odd. To Evie, it suggested something other than a social call was taking place. "Were the men *proper*?"

Miss Wells snorted. "Proper? I'll say they were."

"What do you mean?"

"They were the sort who live in these grand houses. If you know what I mean. But you didn't hear that from me. Not that it matters now. Although…"

"What?" Evie encouraged.

"All these visits, it made us all wonder what went on. As I said, they never stayed long."

Glad to realize she wasn't the only one who'd noticed, Evie made a note of that and underlined it.

Evie asked about the other servants working in the house. There were five women working in the kitchen and five other maids looking after the house. Sofia, Alina, Mischa, Natalya and Sasha.

Evie didn't want to jump to conclusions, however, the names seemed to confirm Mrs. Colliers' background.

"Is there a housekeeper?"

Daisy shook her head. "Mrs. Colliers liked to run things herself. She would give orders in the morning and everyone knew she didn't like to repeat herself."

"And what happens now that Mrs. Colliers is dead?" Tom asked.

"We have our wages for the month. A solicitor came this morning and he told us to stay until then. He left saying he would return to catalogue everything."

Evie assumed he had been charged with disposing of the items and closing the house or selling it.

"How did you come to work for Mrs. Colliers?"

"I worked for the previous owner. He died of a heart attack and Mrs. Colliers asked me to stay on because I knew all the tradesmen and how things were done in the house."

A practical idea, Evie thought. It also suggested a desire to retain some sort of status quo, to keep things as they had been and not stand out.

"Did Mrs. Colliers speak with an accent?" Tom asked.

Daisy nodded. "Quite thick. She said she was from the north." Daisy's grimace suggested she hadn't been convinced, or rather, she hadn't been fooled.

Focused on engaging the maid to talk, Evie had almost forgotten to ask that one key question.

Were the rumors about Mrs. Colliers true?

How had they spread and had they reached the household?

"Did you ever notice any of the men who visited speaking with the same accent?"

Daisy tipped her head back. "There was one… Let me think. Yes, he always stayed the longest. And they argued but not angry like."

"What do you mean?"

"They never raised their voices but their voices hardened. Not really in an angry way but in a firm, mocking tone and then it would soften and they would speak in hurried tones."

"Did the other men who visited her speak in the same way?"

Daisy shook her head. "Those conversations were more casual and muted."

Noticing the young woman frowning, Evie asked, "Did you notice something else about those conversations?"

"Strained. Yes, that's what they sounded like. Almost like they talked but they didn't want to talk. You know, they asked how she was but you could just tell they didn't care one bit how she was doing."

Evie wondered how the maid had managed to overhear those conversations. An ear pressed to the door, she supposed and turned her focus to identifying the men.

"When those men came to visit, did they announce themselves by name?"

"Never. They only ever said they were expected."

Evie exchanged a glance with Tom and wondered if he might be entertaining the same idea.

Had one of those men been Lord Barton?

Had they found a connection?

Lowering her voice, Evie asked, "Can you tell us what happened? I understand you were the one who found Mrs. Colliers. You said you'd been in the dining room…"

To Evie's relief, Daisy Wells didn't need further encouragement.

"Yes. I was about to go down to the kitchen and I walked right past the library. Something looked odd. So I went back and that's when I noticed the door was closed. Mrs. Colliers always had it opened because she liked to bellow out orders. It was odd because I'd heard Miss Smith leave. So the door should have been open. I pressed my ear to the door and didn't hear anything. At first, I told myself to mind my own business. But then I convinced myself it was my business because if I noticed something odd and didn't do something about it, then I would get into trouble."

Daisy Wells stared straight ahead, her eyes not blinking. "I eased the door open. I don't remember if I knocked. I could hear my heart beating in my ears. Then everything happened so quickly. I peered in and saw Mrs. Colliers sitting at her desk, slumped against the chair, her head tipped back, her mouth gaping open and… and her throat slit from ear to ear. I don't know if I screamed. Maybe not because I clamped my hand over my mouth and rushed out of the library."

Mrs. Colliers had been sitting at her desk.

"What did you do next?" Tom asked.

"When I recovered, I went back to the library. That's where the telephone is."

"And that's when you telephoned the police?" Evie asked.

"My hands were shaking. I think I stood at the door looking in for a moment. It suddenly occurred to me there might be someone in the room so I grabbed a fire poker and had a quick look around behind the curtain and the door." She winced. "There was so much blood. It was dreadful. I had to lean over the desk to reach the telephone. It normally sat on the right-hand corner. Mrs. Colliers must have been about to place a call because it was close to her. That's when I remembered Merrin Smith."

Evie frowned. While she didn't wish to interrupt the flow of information, she needed to clarify something. The other visitors had not announced themselves, yet Daisy knew Merrin's name. "Did she introduce herself as Merrin Smith?"

"Sofia answered the door. She was expecting someone else. She's the only one who recognized all the visitors and didn't need to ask their names. But this one... she wasn't expected, so Sofia asked."

"And did she let her in straightaway?"

"No. Sofia went in to have a word with Mrs. Colliers who then agreed to see Merrin Smith. Mrs. Colliers sounded angry. She didn't like surprises. Everything had to be done the way she liked it."

Yet the men had not announced themselves. "Did Mrs. Colliers always know whom to expect?"

"Oh, yes. She had a list. Every week, she would put a cross next to a name confirming they had visited. I know that because several times I walked in to the library directly after one of the men had left and I saw her ticking the name off."

"Miss Wells, do you know where this list is?"

"In her safe."

"Did you tell the police about this?"

"They didn't ask."

Was it possible the police had not opened the safe?

"Do you know if the police took anything away?"

Daisy nodded. "She kept a journal on her desk. I saw it opened once when I took in a tray. It was all gibberish."

If her suspicions were correct, Evie thought it must have been written in Cyrillic and if the police had taken it away, they must have translated it by now or they might still be in the process of doing so.

"Miss Wells, what happened after you placed the telephone call to the police?"

"I stood still, staring at her and then... I've heard stories about spirits lingering. I remember thinking about it and then I couldn't move. I just looked around me and I whispered her name." Daisy lowered her voice to a whisper. "Mrs. Colliers? Are you still here?"

Evie thought Daisy must have gone into shock. She sat still, her eyes wide and not blinking.

"Did she answer you?" the reporter asked.

They all looked at him as if he'd just uttered something silly.

"I strained to hear," Daisy explained. "Just because you can't see or hear something doesn't mean it's not there. I told her to give me a sign and I assured her I was listening."

Evie held her breath.

Miss Wells straightened and shook her head. "Nothing. She said nothing. Maybe she had already moved on."

"What about the other servants?" Tom asked. "When did they become aware of the situation?"

Daisy looked up at him, her eyes slightly widened, almost as if she'd been relieving that moment when she'd tried to engage Mrs. Colliers' ghost in conversation. She relaxed her shoulders and sat back.

"Let me think… Oh, the police arrived. That's when word spread around the house."

"Who answered the door?" Evie asked.

"I did. When I heard the hard thump on the door, I jumped into action. They actually startled me and I rushed out of the library and nearly threw myself at the door, hurrying to open it." She closed her eyes for a moment as if trying to remember something. "Yes, that's when I screamed."

"What did you say?"

"*She killed her. She killed her.* They already knew that because I made sure to tell them when I telephoned. The constables rushed inside and went straight to the library. One stood at the front door and wouldn't let me leave the house."

"So you actually tried to leave?" Evie asked.

"Yes. I suddenly realized what had happened. Someone had killed her and I could be next."

"Why did you think that?"

"Because… because you don't kill someone unless you have good reason to do it, but then… if you kill someone, you must be mad." She gave a vigorous shake of her head. "I don't know. By then, I didn't know what to think but I know I was thinking. Not like when I first found her. That was shocking and I probably felt numb. It's what happens when you hear bad news. At first, you're in shock and then you start asking questions and wondering."

They all nodded in agreement.

"More police arrived. I went to one of the windows, opened it and peered out. I saw them taking Merrin

Smith into custody. She'd made it as far as the end of the street. She must have been so sure of being able to escape..."

"Where were the other servants?"

"Cowering. One hid in a closet. She thought we were all going to be murdered. The kitchen servants tried to leave by the back door but the police stopped them."

"And what about Sofia?"

"She'd been upstairs, in Mrs. Colliers' room sorting through her dresses for the evening. She hid under the bed. Two of the policemen went around the house and got everyone to sit in the front drawing room."

Had the police considered them suspects or witnesses? "How did they react?" Evie asked.

"They were all wide-eyed and nervous. If you ask me, they're suspicious of the police."

That didn't surprise Evie. If, as she suspected, they all hailed from the same place as Mrs. Colliers, then they might have lingering memories of the revolution and an understandable mistrust of anyone in positions of authority.

"What happened next?" Evie prompted.

"A man in a suit arrived. At first, we all thought it was one of Mrs. Colliers' visitors because he looked like one of them."

Detective Inspector Evans. Or, rather, Lord Evans.

Evie frowned. "Had you seen him before?"

"No. Like I said, he just looked the type. You know... not regular like the rest of us. Then he introduced himself and that's when we knew for sure he wasn't one of the visitors. The detective looked around the house and then went into the library. He spent a long time in there. One of the policemen took photographs. When they took Mrs. Colliers away, we all gasped." Daisy surprised them by giggling. "The sight of Mrs. Colliers being taken away in a stretcher with a blanket covering her from head to toe was dreadful, but the way we all reacted was actually funny because we all gasped at the same time."

"Did the detective question everyone?"

Daisy nodded. "One at a time. He called us into the dining room. He wanted to know where everyone had been and what they'd heard or if they'd seen something or someone. When it was my turn, he took me to the library and asked me to see if I noticed anything missing. He did the same with Sofia. We're the only two who ever went into the library. I only noticed the journal wasn't on the desk but the detective said he had it. I told him everything I told you."

So the detective knew as much as they did. Although, he had possession of the journal. Would that yield anything of interest? Most importantly, would he share the information with them?

Tapping her finger on her notebook she held on her lap, Evie realized the detective didn't know everything.

Daisy Wells had not told him about the list of names or the safe.

CHAPTER 15

Merrin Smith had been the only person to visit Mrs. Colliers that day. If no one else had come to the house, then she must have killed Mrs. Colliers...

Evie frowned. Was that how the police viewed the situation?

Merrin Smith had not been expected. Sofia, the maid who usually answered the door, had been expecting someone else.

Evie shook her head as if trying to disperse the thoughts and clear her mind.

She still struggled to believe Merrin capable of killing someone. In fact...

"Merrin Smith could not have killed Mrs. Colliers," Evie whispered as the gruesome details of the scene sprung to mind.

Daisy Wells received her fee for the information she'd supplied and the reporter offered to drive her back but she turned down the offer, saying she had some shopping to do and needed to take her mind off, although, heaven help her, she'd never forget what she'd seen.

"Should we go somewhere to talk about all this?" James Peters asked.

Evie and Tom nodded.

The reporter swirled around and then pointed toward South Kensington. "The Zetland Arms pub."

Tom noted the address and they drove there.

"Any thoughts, Countess?" he asked just before they arrived at the pub.

"I want to say I'm feeling rather pleased with the amount of information we now hold." Evie opened her notebook, turned a page and, skimming through the contents, she set it aside.

"But you can't really mean it because we haven't made any sense of it all," Tom offered.

She agreed with a sigh.

Who were all those men who'd visited Mrs. Colliers so regularly?

"But you didn't hear that from me," Evie said.

"What's that?" Tom asked.

"Miss Wells said that about the men when she described them as being the type who belonged to the upper echelons."

"Oh, the ones who live in the grand houses."

"Yes. I assume Miss Wells, along with the other servants, were not to talk about the men who visited Mrs. Colliers to anyone outside the house."

Tom smiled at her. "I believe your brain is churning the information."

"It has been a productive morning and I can't imagine getting any rest until we find some sort of connection.

Then, there's the matter of Wilfred Greer turning up as he did in Lyall Street." She looked at her wristwatch. "We should have some luncheon and get to work straightaway. With any luck, the others will have found something wonderfully entertaining and won't return until much later in the day." Rolling her eyes, she remembered seeing the Duesenberg driving along Lyall Street...

Tom brought the roadster to a stop. "I'm sure the Zetland has some nice pies."

Evie laughed. "Yes, of course. I'd never come between you and your favorite food."

James Peters waited for them by the door. Evie put on her polite smile but she still couldn't bring herself to trust him.

"It's still early," he said. "Plenty of tables."

He led them in and they settled in a corner table away from the bar.

Leaning forward, he clasped his hands. "Well? What did you make of all that?"

Evie had a few ideas but she was reluctant to voice them because they hadn't quite taken shape.

"What do you think?" she asked.

The reporter shrugged. "You've met the suspect. Do you think her capable of such a crime?"

"I couldn't say for sure because it's possible for people to be driven to do something they would never dream of doing. The question I'm entertaining is whether or not she is capable, as in, physically capable of slitting someone's throat. I imagine there would be a struggle and Merrin is quite slim."

Tom nodded. "The way Daisy Wells described the scene leaves a lot in doubt. Mrs. Colliers would have been sitting at her desk and someone sneaked up on her. I can't think how someone would slit a throat while facing their victim. I can't even imagine Mrs. Colliers allowing someone to get that close to her. It sounds as if she used the desk as a barrier."

A seat of power, Evie thought and remembered Daisy saying the door to the library was usually open so Mrs. Colliers could bellow out her orders.

The detective certainly had the advantage. He had photographs of the crime scene.

"Again, despite all we now know, we don't really have enough information," Evie mused. "How do we know Mrs. Colliers was really sitting down? She could have been posed on the chair."

Again, Tom agreed. "But that would require some strength."

Evie hummed under her breath. "A photograph would indicate the location of the greatest amount of blood. Without facts, we can only come up with a vague theory."

The reporter made a note of that and asked, "What about motive? Why did Merrin Smith go to Mrs. Colliers' house? She'd never been there before."

Evie thought of Lady Barton. What if Merrin had gone to the house on her behalf?

She tried to remember if she'd mentioned Lady Barton to the reporter. It seemed safer not to. Although, she admitted, highly unfair. She knew she was extending Lady Barton a courtesy by keeping her name out of the conversation. While she had shared the name with the detective, she remained reluctant to provide the name to the reporter who might be only too happy to use it for his newspaper column.

James Peters answered his own question, "Maybe Merrin Smith was one of those not quite proper women. And what do you think those women actually do?"

Tom and Evie shrugged. Although, Evie suspected Tom had a very clear idea taking shape in his mind.

James Peters sat back and glanced around the pub. "Something doesn't quite fit the picture."

"I agree," Evie said because she didn't want to make her silence too obvious.

"What were you trying to determine by asking about the spelling of Sofia?" he asked.

Evie looked down at her hands. Deciding to share the information, she said, "There's a rumor floating around about Mrs. Colliers real name being Ratchenko."

"That sounds foreign. Is it Russian?"

"We think it is. If she'd hired servants from her motherland, we might confirm that theory."

He gave an impatient nod. "And what about that fellow we saw in the street? I know him from somewhere but I still can't pin him down."

"Mr. Peters, did you take part in the war?" Evie asked.

He winced. Nodding, he said, "Right in the thick of it, at the Somme."

Evie glanced at Tom in time to see him produce a similar wince.

"It's possible you might have seen him in the trenches," Tom murmured but didn't mention seeing him the previous day or at the club.

It seemed Tom shared her suspicions about the reporter or, rather, lack of trust.

"What's your interest in this case?" Evie asked.

Shrugging, he said, "I'm a reporter. I want to get to the

bottom of the truth. My instinct tells me there is something big here."

He might be right, Evie thought, and the something 'big' he referred to would look just perfect on the front page of the newspaper.

He checked his watch. "At this point, I either dig my heels in and stick with this, or I go hunting for another story."

Evie leaned in and murmured to Tom, "We need more information about Ratchenko."

Nodding, he said, "You could look into the rumors about Mrs. Colliers. It might lead you to someone with an agenda." He provided him with more information about the rumor, mentioning the theft of jewels and the betrayal.

The reporter grinned. "That definitely sounds like a solid motive. I'll see what I can dig up."

To Evie's surprise, he thanked them and stood up. "I'll follow that thread and see where it takes me. Hopefully, straight to motive and to the killer."

They watched him leave, both feeling somewhat puzzled.

"I thought he was going to wring as much information out of us as he could," Evie said.

"We didn't exactly open up to him. I'm sure he sensed our restraint. Either he lacks persistence or he actually picked up on something and is now following it on his own."

Evie scoffed. "That wouldn't be fair."

"Yes, how ironic. Let's order lunch."

CHAPTER 16

On the way back to Woodridge House...

Mrs. Colliers was visited on a regular basis by gentlemen. The words streamed across Evie's mind and she tried her best to hammer out a reasonable theory.

Tom glanced at her. "You're entertaining an idea."

Nodding, Evie made her first suggestion, "If you change the name from Mrs. Colliers to Madame Colliers, how would you interpret everything we know?"

Tom drummed his fingers on the steering wheel. "Gentlemen visited on a regular basis but didn't linger. Women who weren't quite proper also visited on a regular basis and didn't linger. We can't assume Mrs. Colliers was carrying on some sort of sordid business in her house. It would have to be elsewhere."

"I agree. Do you think she might have organized

something? Just so we are on the same page, I am indeed referring to the services offered by madams."

"Yes, but if we come to that conclusion, we'd have to figure out why those men and women visited her."

Evie gave it some thought. "Mrs. Colliers liked to be in control. Daisy Wells said so. She didn't have a housekeeper and she kept her library door open so she could bellow out orders. What sort of control do you think she wielded over those men?"

"If we are to assume Mrs. Colliers was a madam, the men availed themselves of certain services provided by the not so proper women."

"That's right but they're not just men, Tom."

He nodded in agreement. "Society men. Prominent men with a lot to lose if their secret became public."

Evie stilled, her thoughts fixed on one word. "Blackmail? You think the men were being blackmailed?"

"It's a possibility."

Evie thought about the rumor Lotte had told them about. Ratchenko had offered to help her employer only to end up using her as a mule to carry what must have been large amounts of jewels. Killing her, if true, would be quite evil.

"I can actually picture it. Not only was she extorting money from them but she was forcing them to... to what? Pretend they were friends? Or enforcing her control over them? If it was blackmail, maybe she enjoyed seeing them squirm."

Tom brought the roadster to a stop outside Woodridge House.

"Apart from the obvious reasons for blackmail, what other information could she have used against them?"

Evie asked. The men might have been carrying on behind their wives' backs, giving Mrs. Colliers the power to blackmail them, but what if there was something more sordid going on?

"We'd have to know who the men were," Tom suggested.

And how would they get that information? Evie remembered the journal found in Mrs. Colliers' library. The one currently in the possession of Detective Inspector Evans.

She gave a firm nod. "I believe she would have written those names down." In the next breath, she said, "Lord Barton. This time, I'd be happy to bet a pound on his name being in that journal."

Tom snorted. "I wouldn't bet against it because I'm sure I'd lose."

It would make sense, Evie thought. Lady Barton had been quite evasive about her husband. Perhaps they were about to travel in order to avoid *a scandal.*

She looked at her wristwatch. "I suppose we should go inside. We're just in time for afternoon tea."

The drawing room

Edgar greeted them at the door.

"Edgar, did anything happen during our absence?" Evie asked and turned to Tom. "I don't believe I've ever asked that but it's almost been too quiet at home."

Taking her coat, Edgar said, "Nothing unusual, my

lady. Although… Well, as it happens, Lady Evans' luggage arrived."

Evie did not care to comment on the subject. Nodding, she asked, "And did Holmes behave himself?"

"He's currently napping in front of the fireplace in the drawing room, my lady."

That didn't actually answer her question. If anything had happened, Evie assumed Edgar was happy to report all was well that ended well, particularly if Holmes was enjoying the sleep of the innocent.

"And the others? Are they all here?"

"All except Millicent and Lady Evans. I believe they are performing a task."

A burst of laughter drew their attention to the drawing room.

"They sound happy." She supposed they would have to postpone any further talk about the case. "I do hope that's a good sign. I'm not sure I could endure being subjected to their silent scrutiny."

As she turned toward the drawing room, Holmes came bounding out. He dashed past them and stopped in the middle of the hall, as if only then noticing them. He skidded a few feet before he regained his balance and doubled back toward Evie.

She scooped him up and hugged him against her. "What happened? Did their chatter wake you up?"

Tom cupped her elbow. "Come along, you're only putting off the inevitable."

"Thank you for looking after him, Edgar."

He inclined his head slightly. "Tea, my lady?"

"Yes, please."

They walked into the drawing room, both displaying bright smiles.

"Here they are. I can't wait to tell you both all about it," Henrietta declared only to be hushed by Sara.

Oh, dear...

What had they walked into?

Toodles stood by the window looking out at the street. She hadn't been keeping an eye out for them. Otherwise she would have moved away.

Sara and Henrietta sat on a sofa opposite the fireplace. Henrietta appeared to be quite eager to speak. She was almost bouncing on the sofa, her eyes bright with excitement.

Evie thought she heard Henrietta whisper, "What is the point to our efforts if we don't tell them about it?"

Evie hugged Holmes closer to her, almost as if she wanted to use him as a shield.

While Tom had walked alongside her, he now stood a step behind her. Was he about to bail out on her? She looked over her shoulder and narrowed her eyes, the only way she could think of issuing a warning.

The message must have been received loud and clear. Tom pushed out a breath and made his way to his favorite spot by the fireplace. As expected, he picked up the fire poker and began poking at the fire.

Distracted by Tom, Evie said, "I take it you all had an eventful morning." Realizing she had just given them a prompt to divulge their news, she rolled her eyes.

"Here they come," Toodles said and moved away from the window.

Evie sat down on the edge of a chair and settled

Holmes on her lap. She assumed Millicent and Caro were about to make their entrance.

When they appeared at the drawing room door, Henrietta clapped her hands. "Did you manage to do it?"

Evie noticed Tom's eyebrows rising in increments. That prompted her to turn and look over her shoulder. Caro gave her a bright smile that spoke of triumph. Millicent carried a basket which she set down on a small table. Digging inside it, she drew out an envelope and held it up like a priced trophy.

When Toodles sat between Sara and Henrietta, Evie understood they were ready to reveal their news.

Henrietta looked at Sara. "Am I permitted to speak now?"

"By all means. You may proceed."

Evie didn't know if she should shift to the edge of her seat or slip back and settle in to hear their tale.

Waiting until Millicent and Caro sat down, Henrietta cleared her throat. "Evangeline, we had the most marvelous adventure. You'll never believe or imagine what we did."

"You're drawing it out. You promised you wouldn't," Toodles chastised.

"My dear, there is the right way to tell a tale and the wrong way. Anticipation is key to this tale."

Evie settled back in her seat, her lips slightly parted.

"Milady," Millicent broke in. "I feel I should apologize."

Oh, dear…

"Nonsense, Millicent. We ensnared you and forced you to tell us." Henrietta shifted as if intending to get up only to change her mind. She looked at Evie and nodded.

"Despite all your efforts to keep us in the dark, we now know everything."

"You do?" Evie managed.

Henrietta nodded. "We know about Mrs. Colliers."

Sara snorted. "After all the practicing you did, you got it wrong. You were supposed to begin your tale with Merrin Smith."

"Yes, of course. We also know about her."

Evie gasped. "That was you in the Duesenberg driving along Lyall Street."

Henrietta nodded. "We didn't mean to follow you. Well, not really. After all, we had promised never to do it again. Anyhow, we simply couldn't resist. After we extricated the truth from Millicent, we went to Lyall Street and invited ourselves into Mrs. Colliers' house."

Evie's voice hitched. "How on earth did you manage to do that?"

Henrietta tapped her nose. When she spoke, her eyes brightened. "We bribed our way in."

Sara nodded. "Henrietta had the bright idea of saying we were voyeurs and quite intrigued by murder scenes."

Evie gasped again. "Voyeurs? Are you sure you wish to describe yourselves as voyeurs?"

"Evangeline, don't look so surprised. Not long ago, people used to charge admission into houses where crimes had been committed. People love this sort of entertainment. Going further back, a day's outing included a visit to bedlam to see the mad people."

"Entertainment?" was all Evie managed to say.

"Oh, don't sound so disapproving. You do it too but under the guise of investigating."

Evie gasped yet again. "I do not. Oh, never mind all that."

Henrietta nudged Toodles. "She's changing the subject because she knows I'm right."

"Nonsense. In fact, I insist we remain on point. What exactly did you do?"

Henrietta looked at Tom. "We availed ourselves of a certain item which happened to be lying about in plain sight. In other words, we borrowed Tom's Brownie camera."

Tom walked to a chair opposite Evie and sat down, his attention pinned on Henrietta.

"I do hope you don't mind, Tom."

"Not at all."

Henrietta gestured to the envelope in Millicent's hands. "Show them. Bring out the proof of our genius."

Emptying the contents of the envelope onto her lap, Millicent revealed several photographs.

Henrietta clapped her hands. "They are images of the crime scene, Evangeline."

Tom and Evie leaned forward.

"You took photographs… of the crime scene?"

"Well, not exactly. As you can see, there is no body, but we were assured that is the very room where the crime was committed. A very nice young woman told us so." Henrietta turned to Sara. "What was her name?"

"Sofia and I still think she charged us too much. I mean, just look at those photographs. As you said, there's no body."

"Sara, if you'd wanted a body, we would have gone to Madame Tussaud's."

"I can't help feeling we've been taken advantage of," Sara huffed.

Shaking her head, Evie expressed her concern. "Henrietta, what if something had happened to you? I'm shocked."

"Nonsense. We were quite safe. Edmonds was standing guard outside, ready to come to our rescue."

Sara shuddered. "Perhaps Evie is right. In the process of coming to our rescue, he might have been ambushed by the killer."

"What killer?" Henrietta demanded.

"Countess, you must admit, they were quite intrepid."

True and she wished the idea had occurred to them. Evie picked up one of the photographs and sat back to study it.

As Daisy Wells had related her story, Evie had tried to form a picture of the scenes in her mind. The photograph showed a desk with a fireplace on the left and two windows on the right. In her mind, she had actually imagined the windows behind the desk.

Daisy had said Mrs. Colliers had been slumped on her chair and the chair in the picture had its back to the windows. Had the police left the chair as they'd found it? If so, the killer must have attacked her from behind.

She held the photograph closer and studied the wood paneled walls. The edge of the panels on the wall just to the right of the chair appeared to protrude more than the other panels.

"Tom, look at this." She pointed to the suspicious looking panels. "Would you say that's a hidden door?"

"I wouldn't just say it, I would swear it was. It looks

just like the wood panels in your library and you have a hidden door. I think you've hit on something, Countess."

Henrietta clapped her hands. "Sara. Didn't I tell you?"

"Tell me what, Henrietta? Your mouth has barely stopped moving since we set off to pursue this madcap idea of yours."

Henrietta lifted her chin. "It wasn't just my idea. We all agreed. You would not have made a very good Victorian, my dear. No sense of adventure whatsoever."

"Birdie, did you find something useful?" Toodles asked.

"I think I did, Grans." Evie sighed and decided there was no longer any point in keeping them all in the dark. She proceeded to tell them about their quest to find answers from one of the maids.

"That much information must have cost you a pretty penny," Sara exclaimed.

"Actually, it didn't cost us anything. The reporter took care of it." Evie continued studying the photograph. To her delight, she saw a small painting hanging behind the desk. It resembled a religious icon popular in Mrs. Colliers' motherland.

Looking at Caro, Evie decided they needed to speak with Detective Inspector Evans. How would she feel about that?

She looked at the other photographs and asked, "Is there one of Sofia?"

Henrietta shook her head. "No, she wouldn't allow us to photograph her."

"Milady," Millicent murmured.

Looking up, Evie saw Millicent holding a photograph

close to her eyes and studying it with great intensity. Lowering it, she pointed to the corner of the image.

"I think that's the maid's reflection in the mirror. She was standing by the door and it must have been directly opposite."

The young woman had a blank expression. Evie imagined she had stood by, her eyes not blinking. Almost as if her thoughts had been far away.

Daisy had told them Sofia always answered the door. She'd also said Sofia had been expecting someone. Evie assumed the maid could easily identify all the visitors by sight alone.

They would have to return to Mrs. Colliers' house and have a chat with Sofia.

"Where do you think she kept the safe?" Tom asked.

"Hard to say. It could be on the other side of the desk but that's not visible in the photographs. Or it could be hidden behind a panel on the walls."

Edgar entered the drawing room and set a tray down on a table. Standing tall, he announced, "Detective Inspector Evans, my lady."

Caro gasped and swung around toward the doors.

CHAPTER 17

The drawing room

Detective Inspector Evans walked in to the drawing room, his steps confident and filled with purpose, until he saw Caro. He missed a step and nearly stumbled.

He straightened and stared at Caro, his eyes displaying a mixture of emotions.

The detective took a deep swallow. "Caro."

Caro lifted her chin and greeted her husband. "Henry."

Evie's first instinct was to ask everyone to leave the drawing room so the detective and Caro could have a moment alone to sort out their differences. Although well-intentioned, she realized a moment wouldn't be long enough to unravel their problems and find a feasible solution.

Evie decided to take her cue from Caro and the detective.

Out of the corner of her eye, she saw Millicent collecting the photographs and placing her hands over them.

Henrietta, Sara and Toodles watched with interest. While Tom, clearly eager to be somewhere else, had picked up a photograph and was studying it with undiluted interest.

"Detective," Henrietta smiled. "Do sit down and join us. We're about to have tea and I'm sure Edgar has included a delectable cake to tempt us."

Evie straightened. "Yes, of course."

The detective patted his pockets, as if searching for something.

Evie wondered if he would suddenly decide he'd left something vital behind and needed to leave straightaway.

Henrietta sighed and shook her head. "Detective, you should know—"

Sara jabbed Toodles who in turn jabbed Henrietta with her elbow.

Henrietta looked at Tom who sat near her.

Noticing this, Tom leaned away from her.

It seemed the jabbing would end with Henrietta.

"My lady?" the detective prompted. "You were about to say something."

Henrietta shifted in her seat. "I seem to have been sanctioned. It might, therefore, be best if I remain silent."

Caro took that as a cue to express her opinion. "By all means, Lady Henrietta, do speak up. We are well past the time when women were expected to remain silent."

Henrietta hesitated. "My dear, I'm afraid I am not that progressive."

Evie sighed with relief.

"Then again," Henrietta chirped, "one must keep up with the times. Yes, indeed. As I was about to say before I was… discouraged, detective, we all know."

Evie groaned under her breath. What could Henrietta possibly be referring to? They all knew about his squabble with Caro or about the case?

The detective stilled. Evie assumed he was merely trying to interpret Henrietta's remark.

Henrietta gave him a triumphant smile. "We have the proof."

Oh, dear heavens…

"What Henrietta means to say," Evie began, "is that we are in the midst of a discovery…" Evie floundered.

"Evangeline, what is the point of being evasive if you will eventually sit down with the detective to either share information or extort information from him."

Evie gaped at Henrietta.

The detective appeared to reach a decision. "Yes, well… I do suppose that is the reason why I came here."

He'd never sounded so uncertain.

"Detective, would you prefer using the library?" Evie offered.

With a sigh of resignation, he looked for a place to sit.

Tom stood up and gestured to his chair. "I'm usually more comfortable standing by the fireplace."

The detective sat down and drew out his notebook.

When he remained silent, Henrietta said, "Of course, we could go first. Evangeline, tell him what you found."

That caught the detective's attention.

Henrietta gave her a nod of encouragement.

Feeling as resigned as the detective had a moment before, Evie said, "There's a safe in the library. Have you accessed it?"

"And how do you happen to know that?" he asked.

Evie glanced at Tom. His eyes brimmed with amusement. She knew his game. He would only come to her rescue if she was truly stuck. Meanwhile, he would stand back and watch.

"We spoke with the maid, Daisy Wells."

Henrietta exchanged a look of surprise with Toodles and Sara. "Did we meet her?"

That caught the detective's attention. He pinched the bridge of his nose. "Lady Henrietta, am I to understand you visited Mrs. Colliers' house?"

"Oh, yes, indeed. But don't blame Evangeline. She had nothing to do with it. In fact, she has been trying her best to keep us all out of the investigation."

The detective stood up and walked over to the table to pour himself a cup of tea.

"Lady Woodridge, you say you spoke with a maid."

"She gave us a full account. This is the maid who contacted the police. I believe you spoke with her."

"And she mentioned the safe."

Evie remembered Daisy saying the police had not questioned her about it. "There is actually a list of names. Daisy thinks it's kept in the safe." She stood up and joined him by the table where she poured herself a cup of tea. "Millicent, please show the detective the photographs."

His eyebrows drew together. "You have photographs?"

"I'm sure they are not as good as yours," Henrietta said. "Our photographs don't have a body."

"Detective, I'll spare you the trouble." Evie explained how they had gained access to the house and had taken photographs of the library.

The way the detective's eyes bounced between her and Henrietta, Sara and Toodles suggested he now realized she wasn't the only one meddling in police matters. This was a family affair.

Tom cleared his throat. "Perhaps we should go to the library. There is a large table there."

Henrietta stood up first. "Very good idea."

The others joined her and they all led the way out of the drawing room followed by Millicent and Caro, with Millicent saying, "I'm her ladyship's secretary so I should be present."

The remark caught Henrietta's attention. "I didn't realize we had to offer an explanation," she murmured.

"That's all right, Henrietta," Toodles said. "You can use seniority or senility as an excuse, whichever you feel most comfortable with."

Evie took a sip of her tea and set the cup down. "I'll need my notebook. I think it's in my coat pocket."

Tom led the detective out of the drawing room, saying, "You really can't go against the flow, Henry. I wouldn't advice it. By the way, how is your prisoner?"

"We thought she might be safer in custody."

Walking a couple of steps in front of them, Evie turned. "What does that mean?"

"She might be a scapegoat," the detective admitted.

"Oh, I see. You have finally realized she is innocent."

As she crossed the hall, she encountered Edgar and asked him to fetch her coat. "Actually, I think my notebook is in my handbag."

Entering the library, they found the others congregated around a large table which usually displayed the day's newspapers.

When the detective sighed, Tom smiled at him and gave him a pat on the shoulder.

Signaling to the photographs, Henrietta spoke first. "Evangeline has several theories. I'm sure of it."

Evie went ahead and pointed to the wood paneled walls in one of the photographs. "We think that is a door. If that is the same position you found the chair in, then one can only assume someone came through that door. Someone other than Merrin Smith. I'm guessing she'd already left. Daisy Wells said she was in the dining room and was sure she'd heard Merrin Smith leave. In fact, she saw her leave. Daisy Wells is quite observant. She would have noticed a blood-stained hand. I'm sure it's impossible to slash someone's throat and not get some blood on yourself."

"You seem to be very well informed." Shaking his head, he asked, "What about the safe?"

"There is a list of names. We were curious about the gentlemen making regular visits to the house. It seems Mrs. Colliers kept a list and ticked the names off."

She shared their evolving theory about the men being blackmailed.

"We think one of those men is Lord Barton, hence his exodus out of London. We also think Merrin acted on behalf of Lady Barton."

More than ever, Evie believed Merrin had been sent to make some sort of payment.

"Daisy Wells said Merrin hadn't been expected. I can't

think of any other reason why she would have gone to the house."

The detective didn't look convinced so Evie told him about their conversation with Lady Barton and how she had avoided talking about her husband.

"Do you know anything about Lord Barton?" Evie asked.

The detective drew in a long breath. Looking around the room, he met everyone's gazes. "This does not leave this room. Understood?"

They all nodded.

"Lord Barton holds a position in government."

"Is he privy to sensitive information?" Tom asked.

The detective nodded.

Turning slightly to exclude the others, Tom lowered his voice to a murmur so he could only be heard by Evie and the detective. "Does Wilfred Greer have anything to do with this?"

The detective looked heavenward.

"You seemed to know him or, rather, of him," Tom said.

"It's rather a delicate matter. I can only say he has been engaged to, shall we say, clean up the mess."

That didn't make sense to Evie because they had seen him before any of this had happened. "Oh…"

Tom turned to her. "What?"

"He was tasked with cleaning up the blackmail mess."

The detective nodded. "We were not aware of the other gentlemen. Wilfred Greer only knew Lord Barton divulged certain information to… a certain person and was then blackmailed."

Evie snorted. Putting together the 'not so proper'

women and the services Mrs. Colliers might have been providing, she said, "He talked in his sleep."

Sighing, the detective nodded.

Henrietta cleared her throat. "If you'd rather we left…"

Tom and Evie stepped back to include the others.

The detective tapped a finger on the table. "So… we're looking for a list."

"That means going back to the house," Evie said.

Tom frowned and crossed his arms.

"What is it?" Evie asked.

"The list of names. That could be valuable."

The detective nodded. "If it exists, there are people who would not want it to fall into the wrong hands."

Had they stumbled on a motive?

"Maybe someone decided to put an end to Mrs. Colliers' activities," Evie suggested. "By the way, detective, I believe you are in possession of a certain journal."

He gave a stiff nod.

"Is it being translated?"

His eyes widened slightly. "Not yet. It's a matter of finding the right person to do it."

Just in case the information turned out to be sensitive, Evie thought.

Edgar walked in and handed her the notebook she had asked for.

Thanking him, Evie searched through her notes. "Here's something else. Daisy Wells thinks Mrs. Colliers had been about to make a telephone call."

"I suppose you have a theory about that too," the detective said, his tone carrying a familiar note of weariness.

Evie had heard it once before when Detective

Inspector O'Neil had recognized the futility of his efforts to keep Evie out of a case and had finally come to appreciate Evie's abilities.

"We were thinking this happened after Merrin's departure. The telephone call she had been about to place might have been related to whatever message Merrin had delivered. Actually, detective... When did you learn about Lord Barton's blackmail?"

"When I spoke with Lady Barton. She only mentioned the blackmail. Later, I approached Wilfred Greer and got the rest of the tale out of him. It seems Lady Barton didn't know the full story."

"Well, then... I was thinking Merrin had been charged with delivering a message saying all payment would cease at once."

"And you think Lady Barton had something to do with that?"

Evie shrugged. "Lady Barton might have decided to put her foot down. I imagine these were large sums of money."

"Hence their impending exodus from London," the detective mused.

Evie continued, "I really like this theory because Daisy Wells said the maid who answered the door, Sofia, was expecting someone else. I suspect that someone might have been Lord Barton."

"And, instead of Lord Barton, Merrin Smith showed up." The detective nodded. "This would justify her silence. She is loyal to Lady Barton."

"As any good lady's maid would be," Millicent interjected.

"So there you have it, detective," Henrietta declared. "Hasn't Evangeline performed brilliantly?"

Evie looked up and across the table where Caro stood, her arms folded, one eyebrow curved up. She looked supremely pleased, and she was looking straight at her husband.

Henrietta drew everyone's attention to her. "Of course, none of this has anything whatsoever to do with Lady Evans. No, indeed. She did not have a hand in any of it."

The detective's attention dropped to one of the photographs. Evie stood next to him so she noticed what he was looking at.

The image showed a corner of the room and on the edge of the photograph, Evie could see a hand, its finger outstretched as if pointing. A hand with a distinctive ring. Caro's diamond ring—an Evans' family heirloom.

Whatever he was about to say was interrupted by Edgar's return to the library and announcement, "Mr. James Peters and Lotte Mannering."

Lotte walked in, her head held high, followed by the reporter.

"Well," Lotte exclaimed. "This is quite a gathering."

Evie looked at the reporter and was surprised to see him red cheeked and looking quite cross.

Had Lotte said something to him? They had clearly arrived at the same time.

Recalling the task Lotte had been charged with, Evie said, "Lotte, could I have a word with you please?" Evie gestured to the door, just in case Lotte had discovered the identity of the policeman selling information. In her opinion, that would actually suggest Mr. Colliers was merely a product of Mrs. Colliers' imagination, a prop to provide her with some semblance of respectability.

As they exited the library, Evie heard the detective say his priority now was to find that list.

When they were out of hearing range, Evie said, "We'll have to make it quick, Lotte. I don't want the detective asking too many questions and finding out what you've been up to."

Looking up, she realized James Peters had followed them out.

"Tell her she can't spread the news about," he said.

"I take it that means you were successful?" Evie asked.

Lotte nodded. "Shall I write the name down for you. Sound tends to travel."

"That's fine. We don't need it now."

"So you know who the killer is?"

Heavens. No, she didn't.

CHAPTER 18

They had been so obsessed with collecting information and clearing Merrin Smith's name, Evie felt they hadn't even begun to scratch the surface.

They still didn't know who had killed Mrs. Colliers.

Now, they also had to consider that list of blackmailed people. Either someone wanted to find it and destroy it or they planned to use it for their own purposes.

James Peters smiled.

Rolling her eyes, Lotte snorted. "I suppose young Jamie here knows more than he's letting on."

"In the spirit of cooperation," he said, but couldn't continue because, just then, the detective and Tom emerged from the library.

Edgar handed them their hats and coats. That could only mean they were going out somewhere.

"Edgar, my coat, please," Evie demanded.

Nodding, Edgar rushed to get it.

The detective adopted his look of resignation.

"Yes," Evie assured him, "I am going along. You just try

and stop me." With her coat and hat in place, she asked, "Where are we going? Back to Mrs. Colliers' house?"

They both nodded.

James Peters cleared his throat and took a quick step forward like a puppy eager to join in the game.

Evie pleaded his case. "Detective. He has been rather helpful as well as resourceful."

"Very well, but don't get carried away." The detective looked at Lotte.

The lady detective smiled. "Oh, don't worry about me. I'm happy to stay here. I'm sure I'll be thoroughly entertained."

The detective had his own motor car and offered to take James Peters, while Evie and Tom followed in the roadster.

"That was very bad timing, Tom. James was about to share some information."

"Did he give you a hint?"

"Let me think… We were talking about the list of blackmailed people and wondering who the real killer is." She remembered him leaving the pub with a specific purpose in mind, but she couldn't remember what that had been. "I suppose I can be patient and wait. If the information is essential, I'm sure he'll just blurt it out."

They arrived at the house and joined the detective at the front door.

As expected, Sofia opened the door and could not have looked more surprised to see them.

"I thought we'd answered all your questions, detective," she said, her words carrying the trace of an accent.

Ignoring her remark, he asked to see the library again.

At the detective's request, it had remained untouched,

with the chair still in the same place, its back to the windows.

The safe had to be somewhere in that library.

Evie imagined a large strongbox made of reinforced metal. The detective searched behind the various paintings adorning the walls but found nothing. He joined Tom who was looking at the rest of the wood paneled walls.

Evie studied the bookcase to the side of the fireplace, pulling out the books and knocking on the back of each shelf. Next, she looked around and inside the fireplace. She then turned and swept her gaze around the library. Stopping to look at Tom, she saw the moment he found a latch which opened the panel and revealed a passage beyond.

"I wonder where that leads," James Peters said.

"Only one way to find out." The detective walked through and James followed.

Tom looked out the windows and shook his head. Evie assumed he had decided no one could have climbed through them because they were too high off the ground. Someone approaching from the street would have needed a ladder to get up. He tested the paneled door but it didn't make any noise so it seemed possible someone might have come through them. He stepped inside the passage to inspect the door hinges and appeared to be looking for another latch.

Evie continued looking around the library. She walked around the desk and looked for hidden compartments. At that point, she had given up on the idea of finding a large safe.

For all she knew, she might be looking for a small metal box, something that would keep documents safe.

Going around the desk, she stood next to the chair. The room had a large rug but it didn't cover the area under the desk. Looking down at the floorboards, she tested them with her foot. They felt sturdy. All except one.

Frowning, she knelt down and felt around the floorboard. It was a slightly different length to the other floorboards. Almost as if it had been cut to size. Unable to get her finger around the groove, she straightened and looked at the items on the desk. She found a metal letter opener. It was the perfect implement to nudge loose the floorboard directly where Mrs. Colliers' feet would have rested.

It made sense to have a hiding space she could feel with her feet. From what she'd gathered, the woman liked control.

She finally met with success and managed to lift off the board. Inside the small space, she found an engraved silver box with the top encrusted with semi-precious stones. Lifting it out of its hiding place, she set it on the desk.

She didn't know what made her look up. When she did, she realized it must have been the cocking of a revolver pointed straight at her.

"I've spent the last week searching for that."

Sofia.

Evie had been so focused on searching for a safe, she had forgotten about the maid. It annoyed her. Servants were trained to look invisible, to not be noticed, but she always noticed. She always acknowledged anyone walking into a room or walking by. To be fair to herself, she had been determined to find a hiding place.

It only then occurred to her she must have been left

alone. Had the others been equally focused? Yes, of course. Even Tom, who never left her side. They must have all gone into the passage to find where it led.

"I'll take that, thank you." Sofia gestured with the revolver.

Evie had no idea where she'd been hiding it. Inside her apron?

"Step away from the desk," Sofia ordered.

"You won't get very far," Evie warned, her voice calm. She tried to engage her brain. What could she say to convince the young woman to not do anything foolish?

If she said the house was surrounded by police, Sofia might become desperate and use her as a shield, a bargaining chip. Anything could happen.

Could she risk it?

"Think, Sofia. What can you possibly do with this information? You can't use it. We know who the men are," she lied. "They can lead the detective straight to you."

"Step away from the desk," Sofia repeated.

Without taking her eyes off her, Evie tried to remember where everything had been on the desk. Had she seen anything she might use as a weapon? A paperweight? The letter opener? Where had she set it down? If she threw something at Sofia, she would buy herself a few precious seconds. Could she lunge for the revolver?

What was behind her?

When she stepped back, could she reach for something to use as a weapon? Sofia would be distracted for a few seconds while she picked up the silver box.

The revolver looked heavy. If she could buy herself some more time, Sofia might start to feel the weight, she might lower the weapon or shift it from one hand to the other. She held it with her right hand, if she moved it to her left hand, she wouldn't be able to handle it with the same confidence.

If she ever had to face a similar situation, Evie promised herself she would be better prepared.

Annoyed to be giving in, she took a step back, followed by another. Even if she had something to use, how would she overpower the young woman? This wasn't just a matter of stopping her from taking the silver box. Evie couldn't be sure what she would do once she had it in her possession. What if she decided to shoot her?

Sighing, she took another step. That seemed to satisfy Sofia. She smiled and dropped her eyes to the desk.

Before she could look up again, Evie reached for her hat and flung it straight at Sofia's hand, using as much force as she could garner to turn the lightweight hat into some sort of weapon.

Startled, Sofia reacted by cowering back. During that small window of opportunity, Evie reached for the box and threw it straight at Sofia's face.

Sofia yelped and lifted her arms to shield herself. In the process, the revolver slipped from her hand. At the same time, footsteps rushed toward the library. Evie was already rounding the desk and throwing herself at Sofia. If Tom hadn't rushed in just then, they might have both landed on the floor.

He grabbed Sofia's arms and pulled them back, dragging Sofia against him and leaving Evie to fall on her face.

Yelping, Evie just managed to break her fall with her hands and knees.

"Good timing, Tom." Evie moaned.

The detective and the reporter appeared at the door.

Sofia made a futile attempt to free herself from Tom's hold, something the detective took care of by producing handcuffs.

Tom helped Evie to her feet and settled her down on a chair.

Evie sat in a daze as Tom spoke softly, his eyes filled with concern. She heard the detective placing a telephone call. Soon after, she heard footsteps approaching the library and a couple of uniformed policemen appeared and took Sofia away.

When Evie finally found her voice, she said, "It has to mean something."

"Countess, you're doing it again." Tom could not have looked or sounded more relieved. "You're having a conversation in your head."

Evie shook her head. "When I set the silver box on the desk, Sofia said she had spent the last week searching for it."

Tom nodded. "You had a theory about the killer wanting to take over from Mrs. Colliers by getting hold of the information."

"It'll come to me, I'm sure." She looked toward the paneled door. "Where did that lead to?"

"The kitchen and the back door. The detective found traces of blood on the wall. We thought someone might have come in from outside. I guess we were wrong." He hissed out a breath and raked his fingers through his hair. "I should never have left you alone."

"Well, you did, Tom and there's nothing we can do about it now. Please don't berate yourself. I know you will, but you shouldn't. We were all focused on finding that safe."

Seeing the reporter standing by the door and looking slightly shaken, Evie asked, "James, earlier you were going to tell me something. What was it?"

He gave her a worried smile. "I'm sorry too. I should have known better than to leave you alone. It just didn't occur to me to be suspicious…"

Evie rolled her eyes. "As you can see, I haven't actually come to any harm. My ego has developed quite a backbone. Now, tell me."

He smiled. "Ratchenko is a myth. There's a large community of Russian émigrés and they all know the well-to-do tried to take as many valuables as they possibly could with them when they fled the country. Of course, you can imagine the resentment some of these people feel and they all wish they'd had the opportunity to make off with some of those valuable items. In their hearts, they believe someone managed to do what they can only dream of and over time, many stories have sprung up of someone or other duping their masters out of their wealth. The most popular one is about Ratchenko, the housekeeper."

"Well, Lotte will be disappointed. She was sure Mrs. Colliers was Ratchenko."

James smiled wryly. "Maybe she was. We will never know."

CHAPTER 19

Woodridge House

It had been a long day. Returning to Woodridge House, Evie had sighed with relief.

Merrin Smith had finally been released from prison. Although, the detective had insisted she had been in custody for her own safety.

Evie supposed he had been right in fearing Merrin would be used as a scapegoat. Even prisons were not safe. For as long as Merrin was under suspicion, the real killer would assume they were free but it wouldn't be a certainty. The only way to be safe, would be to kill the accused. Accidents happened in prison. It had been a smart move on his part and she had been glad to hear he'd never truly believed Merrin could be guilty of such a crime.

Evie had only just managed to remove her coat when

the police arrived. They had been on their way to Lady Barton's house to deliver Merrin into the safety of her home. Merrin had asked to stop at Woodridge House so she could personally thank Evie for helping her.

That had been Evie's chance to ask Merrin about her visits to the pub, something Evie had continued to puzzle over. It had struck her as odd because Merrin Smith didn't seem to be the type to enjoy such outings. Indeed, that had been Lotte's observation.

And that's when everything had fallen into place, with Merrin providing the reason for her regular trips to the pub.

When Merrin had left, Evie had rushed in search of Tom to tell him the news. Instead, she had been ambushed by Henrietta, Sara and Toodles and the rest of the day had been filled with one thing or another.

Had she told Tom?

Evie shook her head. Right then, she could only think about snuggling against her pillow. However, there was something she couldn't put off any longer.

The rest of the household had retired for the night. She had knocked on Caro's door and had asked to have a private word with her.

They were both sitting on the settee at the foot of the large four poster bed.

Sometimes, Evie thought, the most difficult conversations were between people who knew each other well.

She struggled to find the right words and Caro looked determined to not help her. To make matters worse, every time she tried to speak, Caro made a remark obviously meant to divert her attention.

"Caro," Evie said.

Caro shook her head. "I've only now realized I don't really care for silk. Would you believe that? As the old saying goes, you can't turn a sow's ear into a silk purse. I'll always be plain Caro."

"You are Lady Evans and you can wear whatever makes you comfortable. As a matter of fact, I happen to prefer cotton. Especially during steamy days. Just as well we don't really have many of those. But that's all beside the point. Caro, does Lord Evans know you have left him?"

Caro thrust her chin out. "He's probably pretending everything is perfectly fine and I will soon come to my senses as if I have lost my senses. I've never felt so full of sense in my life. I made a mistake and I accept it, along with the consequences. I suppose there will be a scandal. Or, perhaps we'll avoid it because I haven't been presented and no one knows me."

"Caro," Evie employed her sternest tone. "Does he know?"

Caro looked away.

Just then, they were both distracted by something hitting the window. As they both turned toward it, it happened again.

Evie flicked the switch on the lamp and the bedroom darkened. They both rushed to the window and stood on either side looking out and down at the ground.

Again, something hit the window.

The street light stood a few feet away from the house and failed to fully illuminate the person standing there. But it was definitely a man.

"I think he's throwing pebbles at the window," Caro whispered.

Frowning, Evie pulled the window open. The man stepped back.

Employing her sternest tone, Evie called down, "What do you think you're doing?"

The man looked up and down the street and then said something she didn't quite hear.

"Speak up. I can't hear you."

"*I want my wife back*," he yelled.

Caro frowned. "Henry?"

"Caro," he called out in a hard whisper.

"What do you want, Henry?" Caro asked, her tone conversational.

"You are to come home with me or so help me…"

"Henry, you'll wake up the neighborhood."

Evie had no doubt all the neighbors were currently stirring awake and wondering what the commotion was about.

"This is not the time or place, Henry. You should go back to your club."

"I am not leaving without you," he hollered. "You said… no, you promised, for better or worse."

"I changed my mind, Henry. You are a cruel man."

"Caro!" Evie exclaimed.

Caro turned to Evie. "Well, it's true." She turned back to the window. "Look at him, making a spectacle of himself. Doesn't he realize he's causing a scandal? Everyone will be talking about this tomorrow. For all we know, there might be a reporter lurking in the shadows taking note of the commotion. Our names will be plastered all over the front page. Lord Evans drags his wife along Mayfair street."

"Caro!" the detective pleaded. Then his voice softened. "Caro, my love. Come down."

Caro pressed her hands to her heart. "Oh, dear. I suppose I should rescue him. But first he must promise." Caro gave a firm nod. "Yes, he must promise not to interfere." Caro leaned out the window.

"Caro, do you think this is the time? Surely you could badger him over breakfast."

"I suppose you're right." Caro straightened. "Although, I don't really wish to give in so easily. Do you think I should empty a jug of water on his head?"

They both fell silent and looked down at the lovelorn man.

Caro sighed. "It would be funny, but rather cruel. I should dress and rescue Henry from his misery."

CHAPTER 20

The morning room

$\mathcal{E}$vie buttered her toast. "I have come to a decision."

"A momentous one?" Tom asked.

"Yes, I suppose it is. I have decided to offer Merrin Smith the position of lady's maid. She has proven herself to be quite prudent and capable as well as incredibly loyal."

"You like her because she put all her trust in you."

"Yes, that too. You must admit, that is a sign of good judgment."

"Have you told Millicent?"

"I'm sure she will agree with me… when I tell her."

"And how does Merrin feel about moving to Halton House? There's only one pub in the village and not that many men her age."

"Oh! I didn't tell you? How is that possible?"

They both rolled their eyes heavenward. Of course, Evie had been distracted by Henrietta, Sara and Toodles. They had all insisted she tell her tale from beginning to end, leaving nothing out.

During the brief chat she'd had with Merrin the previous day, Evie had asked about those trips to the pub.

"Those men she was seen with were nothing but pesky patrons trying to chat her up."

"So why did she continue going to the pub?"

"She was there to meet someone. A deal had been struck between Lord Barton and Sofia. Fed up with the situation he found himself in, Lord Barton offered Sofia a large sum of money if she could get a certain document kept in that silver box. Once she obtained the document, Sofia was to meet Merrin at the pub. He gave her a week, the time left before he had to attend his regular meeting with Mrs. Colliers. Let's call it the walk of shame. He was required to make an appearance and make his payment."

Tom's voice filled with derision. "Instead of seeing it all through, he left town and charged Merrin with the task of delivering the payment?"

"Yes. He assumed it would all be sorted out and Sofia would find the silver box, but she didn't. So poor Merrin had to go to Mrs. Colliers' house and deliver the payment."

"That explains her performance during the interview," Tom said.

"Yes, but her visit put her at the scene of the crime. I'm sure the detective will get the whole story out of Sofia," Evie continued. "She's most likely to have run out of patience and seen the opportunity of earning a large sum of money slipping through her fingers."

"So she killed Mrs. Colliers," Tom said.

"Even if she doesn't admit to the crime, she gave herself away. I'm sure the detective will get a full confession out of her." Smiling, she took a sip of coffee and thought of her hat. "I wonder if there is such a word as *weaponize*."

Understanding her meaning, Tom smiled. "Yes, that was quick thinking, Countess. I'll never look at your hats the same way again."

Evie took a nibble of her toast. Swallowing, she said, "And what of the mysterious Wilfred Greer?"

Tom shrugged. "He seemed to be working on the right side of the law. Now that the documents have been retrieved, I suppose he'll shuffle off to carry out his mysterious work somewhere else. Henry said he had several people in his employ, collecting information for him."

"That would explain the envelope I saw him slip inside his coat when he emerged from the restaurant."

They fell silent and turned their attention to their breakfast.

Looking up, Evie remarked, "Have you noticed, we are having breakfast alone. I wonder if that is going to become a new trend."

"I'm not complaining," Tom said. "But it does make me wonder what they're up to."

"I suppose we'll find out soon enough."

Edgar walked in carrying a silver salver. "This arrived for you, Mr. Winchester."

Tom took the crisp white envelope, glanced at it and set it down beside him.

Even from across the table, Evie could see a familiar emblem on the envelope. "I have been very patient, Tom. Are you finally going to tell me?"

Tom sighed and set his knife and fork down. He studied her for a moment before saying, "My good deeds have come home to roost."

Intrigued, Evie lifted her eyebrows. "Do tell."

"That's just the point. What if I don't wish to tell?" Tom frowned. "Good deeds are not meant to be publicized."

"Tom, what have you done?"

"Something I should have done in absolute anonymity. As the saying goes, hindsight is notably cleverer than foresight."

"To quote you," Evie said, "I'm still in the dark."

Tom shrugged and pushed out a breath. "I diverted some funds and set up a farm for boys who have lost their way. It's near Cornwall. Anyhow, it was all meant to be a simple exercise of giving something back."

"It sounds marvelous. But what happened? Is it not working as you'd hoped?"

"Oh, no. It's working perfectly fine. Somehow, word spread and someone took it upon themselves to reward me for my so-called grand gesture."

"Reward you? Is someone giving a dinner to celebrate your good deed?"

"I wish." His eyes dropped to the envelope. Pushing out another breath, he held it out.

Evie took it and studied it. A thrill of excitement coursed through her. She lifted the flap and removed the piece of paper. As she read, her eyes widened. When she reached the bottom of the page, she looked up.

"Never. *Really?*"

Tom rolled his eyes. "I will never live this down."

"Tom!" Evie looked toward the dining room door.

"Countess. Do not move from that chair."

"Oh, but they must be told. Although, I suppose you're right. We'll have to find the right moment. Oh, this is delicious. To actually know something they have absolutely no knowledge of."

"Now you're starting to worry me."

Evie lifted the letter and read it again. "I've heard of this happening. In fact, that's how William Waldorf Astor received his peerage. Tom, good heavens. A knighthood for your philanthropic activities. When is the ceremony?"

Tom lifted the coffee cup to his lip. Taking a sip, he smiled at Evie. "You mentioned taking some time and going away together. How does a spot of fishing sound?"

Printed in Great Britain
by Amazon